Commander George Gideon has all the qualities which foreigners traditionally attribute to the English—unflappability, a laconic manner and a fair, unprejudiced outlook, which he extends to even the most hardened criminal.
He's tough when he has to be—which is often—and pursues a case with remarkable tenacity.
Which is all by way of saying that he is a damn good copper—and that's why 'Gideon of the Yard' is famous the world over.

by the same author

Gideon's Day
Gideon's Week
Gideon's Night
Gideon's Month
Gideon's Staff
Gideon's Fire
Gideon's Lot
Gideon's March
Gideon's Ride
Gideon's Vote
Gideon's Badge
Gideon's River
Gideon's Wrath

and available in Hodder Paperbacks

Gideon's Risk

J. J. Marric

HODDER PAPERBACKS

First Published July 1960
Hodder Paperback Edition 1962
Second Impression 1967
Third Impression 1971

The characters in this book are entirely imaginary and bear no relation to any living person

Printed in Great Britain
for Hodder Paperbacks, Ltd.,
St. Paul's House, Warwick Lane, London, E.C.4,
by Richard Clay (The Chaucer Press), Ltd.,
Bungay, Suffolk

ISBN 0 340 00879 2

CONTENTS

Chapter		Page
1	Need for Decision	7
2	Whispers	17
3	Pattern	29
4	Duck's Pool	40
5	Argument	47
6	Killer Car	61
7	Borgman	70
8	Birth of Two Criminals	82
9	Grounds for a Charge	97
10	Arrest	112
11	First Hearing	120
12	Bad Day	132
13	Risk	144
14	Missing Men	157
15	Mortimer's	171
16	Second Hearing	182

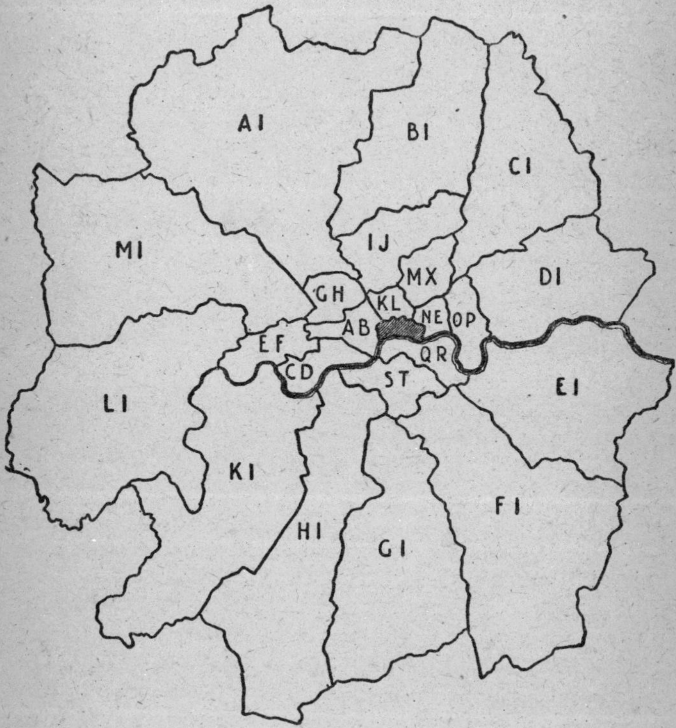

SKETCH MAP OF GIDEON'S TERRITORY

The map conforms only approximately to the boundaries of the Metropolitan and City Police Forces, and the divisional reference letters do not coincide with the real London divisional letters or boundaries

CHAPTER I

NEED FOR DECISION

"He did it all right," Appleby said. "The question is, can we make it stick?"

Gideon did not answer. He sat, massive and pugnacious-looking, with the bright light from the window which overlooked the Thames shining on his thick grey hair, which was combed straight back from his forehead, and on his strong, rather rugged face. The light made his eyes glint, and put one side of his face into shadow.

Appleby, an older, thinner man, white-haired and balding, had just looked in on his way home. It was after six o'clock, and Appleby, near retirement, seldom stayed late these days; the work of Scotland Yard had worn him thin and anxious. He stood with his back to the window, one hand stretched out rather like an orator impatient to make his point.

"If you ask me, it would be a mistake to prosecute, George. You can't afford to risk a not-guilty verdict. We had those two last year, and we haven't stopped being laughed at since. And Borgman's too big. He's got too many influential friends and far too much money. Damn it, he owns a newspaper, a book publishing business, he's in newsprint, magazines, commercial T.V., films—he's the cat's whiskers, and don't you forget it. It's no use telling me that the law for the rich and the poor is the same, either."

In his deep voice, but mildly, Gideon said: "I didn't know I was telling you anything."

"What I say is, it's better to let him go and watch him. If he ever tries again, we'll get him then, even if I'm not here to see it, but the fact that we're watching him will clip his wings."

"Will it?"

"You know it will, George. Here's a chap with everything to lose by crossing swords with us, and nothing to win. What he wants is a fright: scare the wits out of him, and he'll behave himself. Would you like to spend the best part of your life in quod knowing that if you were outside you could spend money like water?"

"I see what you mean," Gideon conceded.

"What you mean is, you don't agree with me," said Appleby disgustedly. "It isn't often I disagree with you, either, but you can chalk this up as one of the occasions. At the most you ought to keep digging and see if you can turn up anything more to make the case stronger; it'll be asking for trouble to go on what you've got now. There's one good thing," Appleby added, almost smugly. "The P.P.'s office will stop you, even if you can persuade the Old Man that you ought to put Borgman in dock. I've spent most of the afternoon going over the evidence, and we simply haven't got enough on him; there are far too many ways he can dodge. And he'd have the best counsel in the country—Percy Richmond, for a fortune. Remember the last time Percy got his teeth into one of our chaps at the Old Bailey—poor old Fred Lee? Fred's never really recovered from it, he's nothing like the man he was —always jittery in case he does the wrong thing, or forgets something. You'd probably have to go in the box yourself on this case, remember."

"Wouldn't want anyone else to," Gideon declared.

"Be a fool if you didn't try to get a stooge," said Appleby. He moved back to the window and leaned against it, his face shadowed against the light, but his eyes very bright; he spoke with unusual vehemence, for obviously this meant a great deal to him. "George, I've been in this dump for forty years. I've seen every kind of mistake made a hundred times. I've felt like hell about some, and laughed up my sleeve at others, but I don't want to see you make a bloody fool of yourself. Bigger the man, harder the fall. It's not only a personal matter, either. If I were to get slapped down, or held up to ridicule by Percy Richmond, or if one of the other superintendents copped it, we would get over it. But you're the great infallible of the Yard—"

"Dry up, Jim."

"Well, that's what the public have come to think, and you know as well as I do that the Yard lives by its reputation. More people associate you with the Department than they do anyone else, and you mustn't take a risk of being smacked down by a smooth-voiced Q.C."

Gideon moved back in his chair.

"Not even if it means letting a murderer get away with it?"

"I could name a dozen killers who've never been tried. What's new?"

"Nothing's new," Gideon agreed, "but I don't want Borgman to go free because he's rich and influential. If he was a poor man, wouldn't you advise me to have a go at him?"

"He wouldn't have a genius to get him off, then," Appleby declared.

"Perhaps not," conceded Gideon, placing his large hands on the desk in front of him, and pressing them down lightly; the fingers were broad and the tips rather blunt, but the nails were well-shaped and well-kept, and the matt of dark hairs on the back of the fingers added to the impression of strength. "I don't know what I'm going to recommend yet, Jim—I've got until tomorrow morning to decide. If I could have a free night for a change, I might be able to decide the right way." He gave his rather slow grin, but there was no smile in his eyes. "You've known the truth for as long as I have, and now there's hope of establishing it. Borgman killed his wife, inherited her money, and married another wealthy woman inside a year. Really want to let him get away with it in case we get a slap in the face?"

"George, if I thought there was a fifty-fifty chance of fixing the devil, I'd give half my pension for it, but the first wife died over four years ago. There's been no real evidence until this last month or so. Now we know for certain that the nurse who attended the first Mrs B. had been Borgman's mistress for a year or more, and continued to be for six months. Then he married the present

Mrs B. and there's evidence—of another nurse who made a statement on her death-bed—that just before Borgman's second marriage his mistress was paid off with a thousand quid, and she hated his guts. She told this other nurse, an old friend of hers, that Borgman had given his first wife an overdose of morphia."

"Trying to argue that it doesn't sound feasible?" demanded Gideon.

"Of course it's feasible, and of course it happened, but all you've got is a statement by an old woman who died just after making it. It isn't even hearsay evidence."

"It's enough to make me want to talk to that nurse who was Borgman's mistress, and could have helped him to murder his wife because she had hopes of becoming the future Mrs B.," said Gideon.

"Nothing to stop you trying," conceded Appleby, "but the nurse emigrated and got married; we don't know her married name—she might be dead for all we know. And even if we found her, we couldn't fix extradition on the strength of what we've got. You're doing what you're always telling us poor mugs not to do—just guessing," Appleby jeered.

Now Gideon grinned.

"Call it a hunch," he conceded. "Jim, you're probably right, and the Public Prosecutor's Office won't go ahead with it even if I could carry the Old Man and our legal department along with me. They'll all agree with you—the new facts don't really strengthen the case. They wouldn't prosecute before and they won't now. But I thought they should have prosecuted even then." He stood up with a single movement, unexpectedly brisk, and looked huge behind the desk, his six feet carrying his great breadth of shoulder well. "That telephone hasn't rung for a quarter of an hour—must be a record. Let me get out of here before it starts. I promised Kate I'd try to go with her to a film tonight." He stretched out for his hat, which was on a stand at one side of the desk, while Appleby stayed by the window, as if he wanted to go on protesting. "Come on, Jim. Let me drive you home, and you can get the rest off your chest on the way."

"It'll just be a waste of time," Appleby grumbled, but he moved to the door, picking up a bowler hat as he went. In the empty passage, his stride was as long as Gideon's, although he looked only half as broad. "You haven't another reliable witness and you've got to face that, George. The doctor gave a certificate—the woman was likely to die anyhow—and once a doctor's signed his name he won't retract. In any case, you'd be asking him to remember details of something that happened some years ago, and old Percy would make hay of him, too."

They were swinging along the passage, Gideon planting his feet down with a thump and leaning forward slightly; Appleby inclined to walk on his heels. A door at the end of the passage opened and a small man hurried out, and stood aside at sight of Gideon.

"Good-evening, sir."

"Evening. Everything all right?" Gideon asked.

From inside the room, a man called: "That you, Gee-Gee?"

"No," Gideon retorted.

"Half a mo'," the caller boomed, and a moment later he appeared at the open door, a middle-aged man with reddish hair and the look of an Irishman, although there was not a trace of brogue in his voice. "Everything's clear in your notes except the bit about Tiny Bray."

"Ever known anything about Tiny to be clear?" asked Gideon.

"Did he say that we could expect that furriers job to be pulled at Leventhal's or not?"

"He said it might. I didn't want the Division warned because we've had false alarms before, and old Hoppy's a bit sore at the moment," Gideon explained. "I shouldn't talk to the Division unless Tiny rings up again, if I were you. Just have a couple of our chaps near Leventhal's."

"Accidental like," the red-haired man said dryly.

"They could have been round to see that Robson woman about her missing husband," Gideon suggested.

"We know that if those furs aren't raided by midnight they won't be tonight—you can work it without upsetting Hoppy."

"About time he was put out to grass," remarked the Irish-looking man, Superintendent O'Leary, and then realised how near Appleby was, and gave an infectious grin. "No offence meant—we could use you for another ten years!"

"Wis there iver sech a man wid his blarney?" riposted Appleby. "Come on, George, or you'll be doing his work for him all night, as usual."

He went on. Gideon and O'Leary nodded, with complete understanding, and Gideon followed Appleby, who had nothing to say when they reached the lift. It was empty, at their floor. Appleby opened it, stepped inside, and then let go a broadside: "If you exhume Borgman's first wife, you'll be starting a load of trouble for yourself, and the rest of us. Why don't you wake up to it? I tell you I've checked everything. You've had three of our chaps and the Division working on this for three weeks, ever since the old nurse made her dying statement, and they haven't been able to dig up anything except the fact that the nurse was Borgman's mistress."

"Keep trying," Gideon urged. "Find out where she went and who she married and where she is now."

"George, what *have* you got on Borgman? What makes you think you could make a case stick?"

The lift stopped.

"He did it," Gideon said simply.

He dropped Appleby near Chelsea Town Hall, and then headed through the thin evening traffic towards Fulham and his home at Hurlingham. He drove, as always, with extreme care because he was so preoccupied. He was a deliberate man by nature, and the range and intricacy of his work as Commander of the Criminal Investigation Department at New Scotland Yard made him think not twice but thrice about every decision he made. His ability to think quickly without becoming careless made him outstanding, although he was the last man to believe that he was exceptional or infallible.

But he knew that he was good at his job.

It was late September. He had been back a week from two weeks' holiday on the Continent, and his face still had some Swiss mountain tan. The holiday had done him a lot of good, slackening a year's build-up of tension. He could have done with twice as long, but it had been the first real break for years. September had been a quiet month at the Yard; for some inexplicable reason it often was; rather as if the men on the other side of the battle Gideon was always fighting also needed a holiday.

Of the inquiries into big cases which had started before he had left England, only one had remained 'live' when he returned: the Borgman case. He had been uneasy about it from the beginning. The old nurse might possibly have spoken without being certain, but death-bed statements were usually reliable, even though they weren't evidence. There was no personal motive for her making such a statement to implicate Borgman and his mistress, a woman now in her thirties, whose name had been Kennett—Jane Kennett. The fact that she had emigrated had been significant; she had apparently tried to get lost.

There was the hazy possibility that she was dead, and if she was, Gideon wanted to know how she had died. Long before the dying statement, the police had been suspicious about the death of Borgman's first wife, without having a hope of making a case. That had rankled in Gideon. No one had given morphine poisoning a thought, though; Borgman's wife had been involved in a serious motor accident, and there had been some reason to suspect that the brakes on her car had been tampered with, and a certain amount of circumstantial evidence that Borgman himself had tampered with them. In those days he had had a chauffeur-gardener, but driven his and his wife's car himself a great deal; and he was a good mechanic. The new information about a morphine overdose had come out of the blue, and was an indictment of the officers who had investigated. Someone had slipped up badly; the relationship between Borgman and Nurse Kennett should have been discovered years ago.

To get confirmation of morphine poisoning, there must be an exhumation; but because Borgman's wife had been in great pain, two doctors had given her morphine at different times. Each would testify to that; so to give the case a strong foundation an exceptional quantity of the drug would have to be found; even if it were, a good defence could put sufficient doubt into the minds of the jury to nullify its importance—unless Nurse Kennett could be found and would testify. Appleby couldn't be more right, but that didn't alter Gideon's opinion about John Borgman, once a poor man but very wealthy since inheriting his first wife's money. He owned race-horses and an ocean-going yacht, was the friend of many people in high places, as well-known as any film star and in some ways better liked. And he was getting away with murder . . .

". . . if I'm right," Gideon admitted to himself, and turned into the street where he had lived for nearly thirty years, since the day when he had brought Kate here, as a young bride. He drew up outside the house, got out, and looked at the woodwork; it could do with repainting; the outside hadn't been done for two years, and, smoke-free zone or not, paint soon became black in London. He was very proud of the house, and liked to keep it spick and span. It was one of a terrace, and the white paint showed up the dull red brick. He pushed open the iron gate, detected a slight squeak, told himself that if he didn't get busy with the oil-can it would become really noisy; then the door opened and Kate appeared. Gideon saw her face light up at sight of him, and that did him good; he wasn't surprised when she said:

"Hallo, dear. The Yard's on the telephone for you."

He gave her a peck of a kiss as he passed, moved briskly along the narrow hall and picked up the telephone, not troubling to try to guess what the call was about. He had come to accept it as part of life that the Yard would find him wherever he was. He was not even gloomy at the thought that this might mean that he would have to go back tonight.

"Gideon," he said.

"Sorry to stop you on the doorstep," said O'Leary, "but there's a job just come in you'll want to hear about. Tiny Bray's been beaten up so badly that he isn't likely to last the night. He's at the North London. They're giving him blood transfusions now."

"Know who did it?"

"No."

"Tiny say anything?"

"No, and not likely to. The Division's got a man with him, of course. If he comes round it'll be for a few minutes, that's all."

"I might nip over and see him," Gideon said slowly. "Hold on a minute." He was aware of Kate going into the dining-room, aware of a car passing outside, but he was seeing the little man who had informed the Yard about a plot to raid Leventhal's in Bayswater; a little mouse of a man with a strange, unhappy history which had turned him into a police informer; a nice little fellow with a pleasant wife. "Mike, someone found out that Tiny squeaked, and we can be pretty sure that this job was done by the mob planning to raid Leventhal's," Gideon went on. "Turn a couple of chaps over to checking the most likely mobs, will you? If you think it's worth it, talk to NE and QR and see if they've heard any buzz. Ask young Christy to spread news of this round, quick. Tiny had a lot of friends."

"Wouldn't like to talk to Christy yourself, would you? He'll eat out of your hand, but bite mine."

"Don't talk nonsense," Gideon said, and added almost with alacrity: "All right, I'll talk to him. Where did it happen?"

"Walker's Cut."

"Was Tiny on his way home or on his way out?"

"Don't know."

"Find out, will you?" asked Gideon. "And if you come across anyone who was near Tiny's place, let me know."

He glanced at the open door leading to the kitchen and could hear the sizzling of the frying pan.

"Thought you were going to take Kate out."

"We all get ideas," Gideon said. "Thanks, Mike." He rang off, hesitated, and was not surprised when he saw Kate coming, tall, very brisk-moving, so pleasant of face and expression. She stopped in the doorway, and Gideon shrugged his shoulders and held up his hands apologetically. "Looks as if you'll have to go alone," he said. "I've got to be on tap. Sorry."

"I'll try and arrange something," Kate said, and there was no hint of resentment in her voice. "Is it bad?"

"Might be."

"Feel like two chops, or one?"

"Two!"

"That means you didn't have any lunch," Kate said. "One of these days you'll suffer for missing meals. Ten minutes, dear." She went off, and Gideon dialled the number of the NE Divisional Headquarters. As he did so, much of what he knew about NE came automatically into his mind. It was the East End Division, a tough one, and Christy had been newly promoted as its Chief Superintendent, largely because Gideon had rooted for him. Some kind of feud was going on between him and O'Leary, and Gideon meant to learn more about it, but there was no hurry. There was the sizzling and the smell of frying chops; there was the ringing of the telephone at NE; there was the mental picture of Tiny Bray, probably in an oxygen tent, having blood transfusions and breathing his last, with his wife sitting by his side and a Divisional detective there watching, in the forlorn hope that he would come round and be lucid enough to name his attackers.

And there was Borgman: a kind of Big Brother, a shadowy face looking down at him, as if in constant challenge. He did not understand the psychological causes, but accepted the fact that Borgman was always with him, a shadow and a scourge.

Then the Division answered, and Gideon said: "Give me Mr Christy, if he's in . . . Gideon here."

CHAPTER 2

WHISPERS

"THAT YOU, George?" Christy was not liked by everyone, partly because he was always a little over-hearty, a little too quick on the ball; sooner or later he would learn not to make other people feel inferior or slow. "You on to the Tiny Bray job already?"

"Just heard about it. Got anything yet?"

"No."

"Tell you what," said Gideon, "spread the story round quick. Dance halls, youth clubs, churches, pubs, the lot. Just say that Tiny was beaten up, don't let anyone think that he might die—as soon as they know it's a murder rap, everyone will close up. If we're going to get a squeak it will be before anyone knows how serious it is."

"Yes. Thanks a lot."

The sincerity in his voice revealed the side of Christy which many people did not know was there.

"Got any ideas?" asked Gideon.

"Almost certainly the mob planning the furrier's job."

"That's what I think."

"Might get a line soon, if we're lucky," Christy said. "I've got three lots of possibles marked out, and I'm checking whether any of them is likely to play it rough."

"How've you planned to handle the house-to-house calls?" Gideon asked, and so implied that Christy already had that lined up.

"Just been thinking about it," Christy answered. "If you're right and some people might be scared of talking, I'd better tell our chaps to promise that they won't divulge the source of information. I'll have the questioning started off with that, it might just make the difference."

"Good," Gideon said. "I'll be in all the evening, unless I come over and see you and Tiny."

Gideon rang off, brushed his hair back with the flat of

his hand, and then went into the kitchen, where Kate was prodding at a thick chump chop, the fork sinking into the crisp, golden fat. She didn't look up. Gideon took off his coat and rolled up his sleeves, washed hands and hairy forearms under the tap at the sink, and was drying his face when Kate said:

"Couldn't you leave a message at the box office?"

"Wish I could," Gideon said, "but even then I'd be on edge and wouldn't enjoy the film. Can't Penny go?"

"She's got her usual date with Frank," Kate said. "Anyhow, she's not coming home tonight; she's playing at a concert near Staines and I thought she might as well stay. You'd never believe how I miss Pru!"

"Well, she's happy enough with her Peter," Gideon said. "Matthew—"

"The children can be ruled out," Kate said firmly. "Are you really likely to go to the hospital?"

"Think so."

"Mrs Templeman across the road said she wanted to see the film. I'll pop over and find out if she can come tonight," Kate said. "Stop blowing like a grampus, and sit down and have your supper." She was putting a huge plate, piled high, on a corner of the kitchen table; they always ate there when they were on their own. She sat down to nearly as large a meal as Gideon and, as they ate, he told her tit-bits about the day's events, and about Tiny Bray.

"I hope you find the beasts who did that," Kate remarked. "Isn't he the one with the sick wife?"

"Yes."

Kate said: "It's a good job you never feel as vindictive as I would."

"Don't I?" asked Gideon, heavily, and they were silent for a while, until Kate asked:

"Have you decided what to do about Borgman?"

"Can't make up my mind."

"Do you still feel the same as you did last night?"

"Be astonished if he didn't kill his first wife," Gideon said, "but I'm beginning to think that I'd be more astonished if we could ever prove it. I wish I knew what it is about Borgman that I can't wear. There's something —" He shrugged, speared a last morsel of meat, gave his slow grin, and said: "I'm getting fanciful."

"When do you have to decide?"

"There's a conference tomorrow morning. Either we exhume the body, and, if we find enough morphia, make a charge, or we put it aside for a couple of months or so. If we could make a charge now, we could have the trial at the next sessions at the Old Bailey. If we wait any longer it will be put off indefinitely." Gideon related more or less what Appleby had advised, elaborated a little and, as Kate cut into a blackberry and apple pie and the aroma filled the room, he asked: "What would you do, Kate?"

"Feeling sure that he had killed her, but worried in case Percy Richmond would make a fool of me if a charge were preferred?"

"Yes."

"Don't be soft," Kate responded, and placed a dish in front of him, then pushed the milk jug close to his side. "You can't make your people charge him, but you'll have to try." She was so matter-of-fact about it that Gideon found himself smiling and felt a lifting of his spirit; she was right: he would have to try to persuade everyone at the conference that they must prosecute Borgman. "Of course you know the truth about you and this John Borgman, don't you?" Kate went on.

"Tell me."

"You're the same type," Gideon's wife said. "You don't let anything get in your way."

That sounded like a cliché, yet there was a lot of truth in it. Gideon had studied Borgman's career closely, and found one outstanding characteristic; whatever he started he finished. Borgman was not only brilliant, he was painstakingly thorough. He prepared the ground exhaustively before making any business or financial move. Was it likely that he would have taken any risks with his ex-mistress? "I'm just repeating myself," Gideon said irritably, and made himself think about Tiny Bray.

Christy's men would already be calling at the houses near Bray's home; would be questioning people in the streets leading to that home; would be trying to get a single piece of information that might lead them to the arrest of the men who had so battered the little mouse of a man that he was near to death.

Gideon was still mulling over what he knew about Tiny when Kate went across to her neighbour; she came hurrying back to say that Mrs Templeman was eager to go to the pictures, and then Gideon went to the door, watched her and a short, plump woman hurrying towards the end of the road. Before he closed the door, he was wondering how Tiny was. Borgman was temporarily forgotten.

* * * * *

Just at that moment, a front door was closing on the other side of London. A scared girl was closing it, and she was also thinking about Tiny Bray. The girl's name was Gully—Rachel Gully.

She lived in a hovel in Nixon Street, Whitechapel, one of a terrace of houses which were jammed close together, like teeth packed too tightly in a narrow jaw. She was only seventeen, she was pale, and but for her large blue eyes and a certain gentleness of expression, she would have been plain. Her thin straw-coloured hair was silky, and drawn back too tightly from a high forehead, which had a small bump over the right eyebrow, as if someone had struck her there, making it puffy and shiny. In fact, it was a natural lump. She had been about to step out of the tiny front room of the house, which opened straight on to the narrow pavement, when she had seen three men standing almost opposite, and two men standing at the doorway of a house twenty yards along the road.

She leaned against the door, a hand pressed against her small, unformed breasts. She was breathing rather hard; excitement and nervousness always brought on a spasm of asthma, but the attacks never lasted long. She heard footsteps in the street, and then the roar of a motor-cycle, but all she could see was the cheap, scratched furniture of this, her mother's parlour, and the door which led to the scullery and the wash-house at the back. There were two rooms upstairs, each small, dingy and dark.

Then she went to the kitchen, and her mother looked up from a twelve-inch television set. Music was coming from the screen, and the picture began to form. The girl looked at it, not at her mother—who was a grotesque version of herself as she might be in twenty years' time. The facial likeness was startling, the bump on the high forehead was exactly the same, even the big eyes were alike; but those eyes were set in a round moon of a face, and her mother had become vast in floppy bosom and sagging belly.

"Mum, the–the police are outside," Rachel burst out.

"Well, what about it? You ain't done nothing they want you for, have you?"

"Mum—"

There was a burst of the drums, then a beaming face appeared on the tiny screen. Gradually it became smaller, until the figure of a man was revealed, dancing and cavorting and swinging his arms to the rhythm of the music.

"Mum—"

"*Don't keep saying 'Mum'!*"

"Mum, I saw them," Rachel gasped out. "I saw the men who attacked Mr Bray. I was just going into the Cut when I heard him cry out. There were three of them, and one of them was Red Carter. Mum, what did I ought to do? The police—"

Her mother jumped up and moved towards her. The screen was talking and there was a background of music and a crescendo of song: *Here Comes Charlie, Good Old Charlie.* The din filled the little room, reverberating against the framed prints on the walls, jolting a huge china dog which was painted a hideous gilt colour. The older woman walked unevenly, floppily, her right fist was raised and clenched for emphasis.

"You never saw anything, and don't make any mistake about it. You never saw Red Carter or anyone else—why, what do you think would happen to you if you squealed to the cops? You just keep your mouth closed and forget all about it. Does anyone else know you know?"

"No! But, Mum, I—"

"Thank Gawd you had the sense not to talk about it," said her mother, in gusty relief. She glanced round at the television: Charlie was now singing on a low-pitched, toneless note, and the music in the background was barely audible. "Now remember what I tell you—you never saw nothing, you don't know anything about it. I don't want no daughter of mine to be a squealer, in any case, and remember what would happen to you if—"

There was a loud knock at the front door. Swiftly, the fat woman turned and dived towards the television, twisted the volume control until the voice blared out again deafeningly.

"Pretend you didn't hear the knock, see. We're watching the telly, and didn't hear—"

"But, Mum—"

"*Pretend you didn't hear the knock!*"

"But, Mum, I saw Red Carter there, and–and it's not fair to pretend I didn't. They've knocked Mr Bray about something awful; the ambulance had to come and take him away. He might even be dead."

"You little fool," rasped her mother, and clutched her shoulder and breathed into her ear, the sibilants sounding even above the blast of the television. "You forget all about it. If it was Red Carter he wouldn't care what he did to shut you up, that's it and all about it. Just keep your trap shut." She gripped Rachel's shoulders and thrust her down into a chair. "No one will think we heard that knock if—"

The knock was repeated, but was hardly audible.

"There you are," she said triumphantly. "You can't really hear it; no one will know we heard."

"But, Mum—"

"Don't keep 'but Mum-ing' me!"

"Don't you understand? They'll come back, it's no use pretending!"

"You listen to me, my girl," Mrs Gully said, with

menace in her manner. "You put your backside in that chair and stay there until the cops have gone. And if they come back, remember what I told you—you didn't see or hear anything. Why, that Red Carter would cut your throat as lief as look at you, and you know it. What chance do you think *you'd* have? If you had the proper statistics, okay, but Red wouldn't be any more interested in you than he would be in a boy, and don't forget it. Just sit down and remember what I've told you."

Rachel leaned back and closed her eyes. She was listening for a repetition of the knock at the front door, but either it did not come, or she did not hear it because of the television's din. Slowly, she relaxed. After ten minutes she began to watch the antics of Charlie, and her mother turned the set down. Neither of them moved until the programme was over, and immediately there was an announcement:

"*Professor Arnold Keven, recently back from a long visit to the excavations near Piraeus, will give . . .*"

"Turn it off, turn it off," said Mrs Gully in vexation. "It beats me why they don't make sure we have a decent programme all the evening. Where were you going when you saw the cops, Rach?"

"To the pictures."

"That's okay, so long as you don't talk about anything you *think* you saw." Rachel's mother winked, all menace gone, then went to a small cabinet standing in a corner, opened it, and took out a bottle of gin. She poured some fastidiously into a cracked yellow cup, tossed it down, gave herself a little more, then put back the cap and put the bottle away. She smacked her lips when she turned round, and gave Rachel a leery smile. "Them that talks least lives longest, that's what I always say. But it's okay, you can go to the pictures."

"It's too late now," Rachel said miserably. "I'd better stay in."

On the words there was a loud rat-tat at the front door. Mrs Gully started violently, hesitated, then pushed Rachel aside and strode across the room.

"I'll send them off with a flea in their ears," she boasted. "Can't let decent people enjoy a quiet evening. We'll see about them."

She opened the door.

* * * * *

Detective Officer Cyril Moss, of the NE Division, was a curious mixture of shyness and boldness, timidity and aggression. His chief quality as a detective had little to do with either fact, but much to do with his exceptional power of observation and his almost photographic mind. He had only to see a thing once to remember it; only to see a face and hear the name of its owner to be able to identify him at any time. He noticed the trivial and the unimportant as well as the vital, and he was beginning to learn how to distinguish between a thing that probably mattered a great deal, and one that hardly mattered at all. He was also learning how to go through everything he had noticed during the day, and place it in the right perspective.

As far as it was possible to be sure, the attack on Tiny Bray had taken place at six thirty. Moss, who had been a police constable on this beat for three years before his transfer to the Criminal Investigation Department, had immediately asked himself who usually used Walker Cut about that time; and, also, who passed it at either end. The Cut was used mostly in the mornings and at about six o'clock at night; by half past six most of the home-coming people had passed. Along one side of the Cut was the wall of a warehouse, along the other the lower wall of one of the houses in Nixon Street. Facing the end that led into Nixon Street was the wall of a church building, dark and windowless at that point. So only people using the Cut were likely to notice anything that happened in it.

Tiny Bray had been coming home from his casual job at the docks when he had been attacked.

With great care Moss went through his mental card index, and recalled those people who often used the Cut about half past six: there were seven, including Rachel Gully. Moss reported this to a detective inspector, who told him to question all the possible witnesses. He had talked to five: only Rachel and an elderly man remained. Moss believed that the man was in hospital, and the station was having that checked. Meanwhile, he went straight to the Gully house.

The first time he knocked, all he could hear was the booming of the television, but he had noticed that the volume was much louder after his knock than before; pretending not to hear was an old trick. He went away, joined in the general questioning of the people in Nixon Street and then returned to Number 17 after half an hour or so.

The television was silent.

He banged on the door, and prepared for a long wait. Out of the corner of his eye he noticed that a little man who lived three doors away was peeping at him through a gap in heavily dyed lace curtains; and he was quite sure that the little man was one of Red Carter's mob, although he doubted whether it could be proved. Everyone in NE Division knew about Red and his gang, but none of them could prove anything worthwhile. Moss simply registered the fact that a man who was attached to the Red Carter mob took special interest in his call at the Gully's house.

The door was jerked open at last.

Ma Gully appeared, a mass of fat held together by a dirty flowered frock, her eyes buried in her flabby moon of a face. Moss knew at the first glance that she had been drinking; gin always went to her head, gave her the colour of beetroot, and made her very excitable.

"Well, what do *you* want?" she demanded, narrowing her eyes and thrusting her face forward. "Caw bless me, if it isn't that walking broomstick Mister Moss. What the flicking 'ell are you trying to break my front door down for, *Mister* Moss?"

"Dry up, Ma," Moss rejoined. "Is your daughter home?"

"No, she ain't," boomed Ma Gully, "and I hope she never will be to the likes of you." Moss saw that she was flapping her left hand behind her back, and was sure that she was waving her daughter away, although he did not actually see the pale little drab who lived here. "Don't come tormenting the life out of a decent, law-abiding girl like my Rachel. If you've got anything against her, say it and get it over with, or else go and leave me in peace."

"I want to talk to Rachel, Ma."

"Well, you're wasting your time, she's gone to the pictures."

"Why don't you save your breath?" demanded Moss. "I saw her when you opened the door. Rachel!"

Ma Gully drew a deep breath, backed a foot, glared, then belatedly swore at him. Rachel came uncertainly from the inner room. Moss, who had not seen her for nearly a year, was surprised at the change in her appearance. She hadn't filled out much but she was no longer drab and colourless. In fact she had on a bright red twin-set that suited her. There was some colour in her cheeks, too, and her unexpectedly large, clear eyes were very bright blue. She moistened her lips as she drew level with her mother, who said gustily:

"No one's going to call me a liar."

"Hallo, Rachel," Moss said.

"Good-evening, Mr Moss."

"*Don't you Mister him or—*"

"Did you come home at the usual time tonight?"

"I–I think so."

"Did the shop close at the usual time?"

"Yes."

"Come straight home?"

"*It's an inshult, that's the only word for it.*"

"Yes."

"Then you got to the Cut about half past six."

"I–I suppose so."

"Did you see Mr Bray—Tiny Bray?"

"*She said she didn't, didn't she?*"

"No–no, I didn't," Rachel answered, but her face was very pale, and her lips seemed to quiver. "I didn't see anybody."

Moss felt almost certain that she was lying; even without her mother's interference, he would have guessed that. But if he forced the issue now, he would have to deal with angry Ma, who was quite liable to become violent if she were crossed, but who would probably fall asleep during the evening. Moss knew practically everything there was to know about the habits of the people on his beat, and especially of the Gullys, because he had always rather liked Rachel. Her father had been a big, kindly oaf of a man, rough and heavy-handed, and Ma had always been too easy on the bottle. Rachel had been fond of her father and frightened of her mother, and it had been truly a tragedy when Gully had fallen down the hold of a ship, and broken his neck.

His insurance had kept his wife comfortably off, by Nixon Street standards, and since her fifteenth birthday Rachel had been earning money at a florist's shop and stall near Aldgate Station; for the first time, Moss noticed, she was spending some of the money on herself.

"Sure you saw no one?" he insisted.

"*You calling my daughter a liar?*"

"Honestly, I didn't," lied Rachel.

"Well, if you come across anyone who happened to see Tiny Bray, let us know at the police station," Moss requested, as if he had given up hope of learning anything here.

Ten minutes later, he was reporting to the detective inspector at the station; and soon talking to Superintendent Christy, a big, mellow-voiced handsome man who was a little too flamboyant for Moss's liking.

"Feel sure this girl saw something?"

"Near as I can be, sir," said Moss. "And Limpy Miles was watching me all the time I was outside the house. He went out two minutes after I left. I can't be sure, but I think he was going to Red Carter's place. I asked one of our chaps to try to make sure, but Limpy dodged him."

Nine superintendents out of ten would have said: 'Which one of our chaps?' Christy simply wrinkled his nose, and said:

"Ever heard that Carter goes after furs?"

"Goes after anything," Moss answered.

"Something in that. I suppose you think it would pay off if you called back at the house later this evening, when the old woman's sleeping off the booze? All right—better put in for a couple of hours' overtime." Christy nodded and Moss went off, with a more favourable impression of his chief than before.

That was the moment when Gideon drew up in his car outside the North London Hospital; the moment when Tiny Bray took a long, shuddering breath and died: the moment when Red Carter, a big, raw-boned man in the middle thirties, with his latest doll, a big-hipped, dark-haired girl named Sansetti, was dancing at the Whitechapel Palais, and saying:

"So Limpy thinks the Gully girl saw me. Okay, he's got to find out. Tell him that—he's got to find out. Tell him not to waste any time, sweetheart."

"He won't lose any time," Lucy Sansetti assured him. She acted as a go-between because she enjoyed the thrill of conspiracy, but she had first become a messenger for Red because she knew that Red had an eye for a figure, and was generous with his money when the time of parting came. Red, by her standards, was the perfect gentleman.

Within half an hour, Limpy had the message; and he knew the quickest way to find out the truth was to get Ma Gully drunk.

* * * * *

Although she would have resented the suggestion, John Borgman's wife, Charlotte, was the same physical type of woman as Lucy Sansetti, having the same kind of voluptuous beauty. But there the resemblance ended. She was quiet and unimaginative, she no longer wanted the excitement of a gay life, perhaps because she had everything she could possibly need—including, she believed, the love of her husband.

She did not dream that he was with another woman that evening.

CHAPTER 3

PATTERN

BORGMAN SAID: "My dear, you look ravishing," and kissed Clare Selby. It was a long, slow, lingering kiss, lips slightly parted, teeth touching, not really painful but giving a hint of the excitement of pain. He let her go. She was that rare thing, a true ash blonde, and quite startlingly attractive; had she not been, Borgman would never have been interested in her. He had seen her in the general office of his printing and publishing business, and had been quick to discover that she was a good shorthand typist. He had arranged for her to be promoted two or three times over a period of twelve months, and no one had been surprised when, his personal secretary having left to get married, Clare had been given the job.

She had soon been installed on the third floor of the Borgman Building, where Borgman himself had a suite of luxurious offices; the rest of the floor was given over to the accountancy and financial activities of his various enterprises. His offices were magnificently furnished, and the desk at which he worked had been acquired at the sale of the fabulous Alston Estate; so had a Gainsborough and a Constable in that same room.

Borgman did not think that anyone in the business knew anything about his *affaire* with Clare. She had a little money of her own, and a small flat in the West End; and nothing could have been more convenient. The *affaire* was in its early days, and he believed that Clare was dazzled by his money as well as by his looks and his suavity. He did not know how long it would be before she began to ask for more than she was getting now—snatched hours here, an occasional run into the country in his Rolls-Bentley Continental, one weekend in a tiny French village on the coast, another in the *Lucretia*, his motor yacht.

She had very light blue eyes and a fair skin without the

slightest blemish. She did not make up too heavily, and was young without being silly or kittenish; in fact she was mature. In some ways she was even more mature than Charlotte, and as he stood back and studied Clare, Borgman found himself contrasting the two women, and being amazed at the great differences between them. Clare, tall, slender, gently curved, fair as the wind; Charlotte, getting a little heavy, dark, olive-skinned, eyes the colour of thick honey. Charlotte was better educated than this girl, but had nothing like the common sense and the intelligence; Charlotte was more animal.

The thought made Borgman smile.

"If you're laughing at me, darling, don't," Clare said, chiding.

"That's the last thing in the world I'd ever do," Borgman assured her. "Shall we stay in? Or shall we go out?"

"Can't we do both?"

Borgman found himself laughing.

"We shall do both."

"And can you spare five minutes for business?" asked Clare mildly.

"Can't it wait until tomorrow?"

"I suppose it could but I'm not sure that it should," said Clare. "It depends on whether you mind being robbed or not."

"*What?*"

Clare laughed. "Yes, it can wait until—"

She broke off, not in any way alarmed, but impressed by the change in his expression. She had seen it often before, and had wondered what would happen if she had to clash with him—or whether his business interests or his wife forced a choice upon him. She had no illusions. Borgman the lover and Borgman the business man were two different creatures, and she suspected that Borgman the husband was different again. The change when she had said 'whether you mind being robbed' showed mostly in his eyes—for the glow faded—and in the lines of his full mouth and square chin. He was not really handsome, but his face was hard and his expression arrogant when in repose.

"What do you mean, Clare?"

"I don't think you're going to like it, darling."

"I'll be the judge of that." He was almost sharp.

"It's Old Samuel," Clare announced.

"Ben Samuel?" He often echoed a word or so, to give himself time to think.

"Your favourite cashier and accountant, darling."

"Are you serious, Clare?"

"I suspected Old Samuel soon after I came to work for you," Clare told him. "He was always a little nervous about certain books and accounts being handled by any-one else, and that's a bad sign in a cashier, isn't it? Since I was promoted"—she said that without a smile—"I've been able to tell him that you want to see all the books and accounts, and I've worked late in the evenings on some of them. He's robbed you of nearly two thousand pounds in the past two years, and probably a lot more before that."

"Are you sure?" Borgman asked harshly.

"I wouldn't risk misleading you, darling."

"No, you wouldn't," Borgman agreed grimly. "Have you any of the account files here?"

"Yes."

"Let me see them," Borgman ordered.

They would not go out this evening, Clare knew; they would almost certainly sit over the table, studying the figures, until Borgman was quite satisfied that some accounts had been falsified and a number of cheques altered, and that there were consistent 'errors' in the petty cash. She knew exactly how this had been done to deceive the accountants; she knew that by discovering this she had strengthened her hold on Borgman. He was brisk and incisive as they studied the accounts, and when they had finished he stood up, poured himself a whisky and soda, and sipped it; he seldom drank while he was here.

"The old devil," he said.

"What are you going to do, darling?"

"I'm going to prosecute, of course. My God! To think that he's been doing this under my very eyes!"

"You can't have eyes all round your head," said Clare

practically. "The other accountants and the sales manager might be blameworthy, but not you. And as I've asked for these files in your name, they'll think you have the all-seeing eye."

That startled Borgman into a laugh.

"Samuel will find out about that," he said.

"How will you deal with him, darling?"

"I shall face him with this in the morning, and send for the police at once."

"He *is* nearly seventy, and he *has* been working with the firm for forty years."

"And for all we know he's been swindling the firm for forty years," Borgman said harshly. "Don't start getting sentimental; there's no room for sentiment in business, I thought you knew that." He finished his drink. "Do you really want to go out?"

She was smiling at him . . .

* * * * *

At the moment when Borgman and his mistress went into the bedroom, an elderly man was standing at the open front door of his small house near Croydon, ten miles away. When he had bought this house, thirty-five years ago, it had been new and beautifully kept, standing almost alone in a country lane, surrounded by nearly a quarter of an acre of garden. Now it looked old-fashioned and ill-cared for. The once trim lawns were over-long, daisies, dandelions and plantains spoiled the grass with their thick leaves, the gravel paths were overgrown. The privet hedge, which he had planted with his own hands, had just been cut; it was the only really tidy part of the front garden.

It was nearly dark.

A girl in her early teens came cycling past, and waved and called:

"Good-evening, Mr Samuel."

"Good-evening, Bella," Ben Samuel called, but he did not seem to know what he was saying, and he did not look after the girl.

He looked ill, his eyes were glassy, and his upper lip

would not keep steady. He was thinking of the fact that Borgman had sent for the accounts which he had falsified, and trying to accept the fact that there could only be one reason: Borgman suspected the truth. Even if he did not, a man with his sharp intelligence would probably discover what had been happening, and Samuel knew that he could expect no mercy.

"And why should he be merciful?" he asked himself. "How can he know—"

Samuel broke off, went inside, and closed the door. A light was on in the living-room, at the end of a flight of narrow stairs. He walked in slowly. His wife lay on a sofa by the window, her eyes closed, her face the face almost of a skeleton, the bones painted with skin. She had been ill, like this, for nearly fifteen years. It was all very well to say that the State paid for sickness; that was only part of the problem. The State did not pay for the house-keeping help necessary to bring up three ailing children, two of whom had died, and one of whom was in a clinic in the South of England. The State had not paid for the expensive treatment he had tried so often for his wife.

She opened her tired eyes, smiled at him, and said in a voice it was difficult to hear:

"You look as if you've got a headache, dear. Why don't you have an early night?"

"Yes, I will," Ben Samuel said. "I'll get your drink, and then we'll go to bed. I've had rather a tiring day at the office."

* * * * *

Gideon, with the Big Brother Borgman shadow at his shoulder all the time, even when he was thinking of other cases, had not even heard of Old Ben Samuel, and did not know that the old cashier was likely to give him a remarkable chance to probe the affairs of John Borgman. Had he had foreknowledge, however, he would not really have been surprised. He had been amazed, in his early days, by some aspects of the gradual unfolding of the pattern of crime and the fight against it, but nothing really astonished him any more. The pattern was continually changing, but was always there. Often two cases overlapped, and even dovetailed. The ill-considered or the unconsidered trifles sometimes developed into key factors. The seasoned pickpocket, caught red-handed, might lead back to the fence, and, behind the fence, to a school of pickpockets working most of London. The shoplifter, caught for the first time and tearfully protesting her innocence, might lead to a corrupt store detective, or to members of the sales staff working together with the shoplifters. The child caught throwing stones at windows or glass doors might be doing it for the thief who was planning to break in.

The shadow of Borgman was less evident this evening. Much darker was that of Tiny Bray. Gideon had been greeted with the news of Tiny's death when he had entered the hospital, asked if Mrs Bray were there, and was told, yes. She had few close friends, because Tiny had lived in that half-world between the law-abiding and the law-breaking, not trusted by either. Soon after their marriage Tiny had been charged with complicity in a robbery with violence case, and had been sent to prison for seven years. His wife had waited, wholly faithful, wholly trusting. Two years after he had left prison, his innocence had been established. The bitterness had gone deep in Tiny Bray, and because he had been framed and made to pay for a crime he had not committed, he had set out deliberately to revenge himself on all who committed the kind of crime for which he had been imprisoned: he had been an informer for twelve years, and had always informed about the same kind of crime: shop-breaking. He had taken police money for the information he gave, but Gideon as well as everyone else who had known Bray believed that he would gladly have supplied the news for nothing.

He had been a reliable informer, too.

But no one had trusted him and no one had trusted his wife.

"I'd like to go and see her," Gideon told the Matron at the hospital, and was led to the private ward which the police had arranged for Tiny. There was Tiny, pale and thin in death, and not truly peaceful. There was his small, plump, mouselike wife, not knowing what to do, and a nurse and one of the Divisional detectives, who had been there with his notebook. This man, grey and elderly, shook his head at a silent inquiry from Gideon.

"We'll help in every way we can, Mrs Bray," Gideon promised, and touched the woman's arm. "I don't think you should stay here any longer. Is your daughter at home?"

Tiny's wife turned round and looked up with her eyes filled with tears, her plain, plump face whiter than her husband's.

"If you would send for her I'd be ever so grateful, Mr Gideon, I would really. She's gone out to Royston to live, you know. Mr Gideon, you will find out who did this to my Bert, won't you? You will find the beasts."

"We shall find them and punish them," Gideon promised.

When he had arranged for Mrs Bray's married daughter to come, and when he had left the widowed woman at the tiny house in Nixon Street, he saw a man whom he recognised vaguely, turning into the street from Walker Cut. This had been opened again to pedestrians, for the photographs had been taken and the place searched for clues. So far nothing useful had been found. Gideon didn't start the engine, but watched the man walking briskly along, wondering where he had seen him before. He wound down his window, and called out as the man approached:

"Detective Officer Moss?"

The man, who was extraordinarily thin but not particularly tall, missed a step and peered into the car.

"Yes, who—." He straightened up. "Mr Gideon, sir."

"You on the Bray job?"

"Yes, sir."

"Got any line?"

"Just going to have another word with a girl who might have seen something," Moss said eagerly. "I can't be sure, but this used to be my beat, sir, and I got to know everyone pretty well."

"I remember that testimony you gave on the Ericson case," Gideon said.

Moss's eyes lit up.

"Very good of you to say so, sir." The testimony had won him his transfer from the uniformed branch. "Well, this girl said she saw nothing but I think she was scared, and her mother's an old bitch who would rather lie herself black than help us at all. The daughter's a nice kid, though. If I'm right, the old woman's sleeping off the booze at the moment, and I hope the daughter will be on her own." He coloured suddenly, and his Adam's apple began to work wildly. "I've come on my own with permission, sir; it was thought that if there were two of us then Rachel Gully—that's the girl—would be too frightened to talk."

"Carry on," said Gideon. "I'll be round the corner—let me know what happens."

"Yes, sir."

Gideon drove on, smiling to himself, and pulled up round the corner. Here was part of the pattern unfolding again. According to the lately retired superintendent of NE Division, Moss had an extensive and exceptional knowledge of the people on his beat, and could soak up anything he noticed like a sponge. But he had not yet learned to extract the juice of evidence from reports or formal written statements; he had to see before facts registered, and the old Chief had said that, given ten years, there wouldn't be a better man in the Force.

Moss was likely to find promotion difficult because of his scraggy figure and that Adam's apple, though; noticeable Adam's apples and authority seldom went together. Gideon took out his big, rough-bowled pipe, and began to fill it; and took a long time pressing the tobacco down, and was finicky with the little strands which hung over the bowl of the pipe. He saw an elderly man with silvery hair come out of one of the tiny houses: that was Freddy Wayne, who had spent twenty of his sixty years in prison and was almost certainly getting ready to go back again: he was a forger, and sometimes seemed to forge for the love of it.

Funnily enough, Freddy's only son was a leading light in the Salvation Army, who was ready to bend over backwards in order to try to undo the harm his father had done. Gideon was thinking of that, and wondering whether Borgman would have been difficult had he had a son, when he saw Moss hurrying round the corner. Even in the movement of Moss's legs and feet, which Gideon saw first, there was a hint of alarm.

Moss came up, breathing hard.

"I'm a bit worried, sir. Would you mind putting a call out for Rachel Gully?"

Gideon moved forward in his seat almost before the request was made, and flicked on his radio; immediately, the teeming ether woke to life. He recognised the voices of three men on the air, picked up reports on some of the night's crimes, then pushed the switch over again, and said: "Gideon calling Information, urgent, please." He pushed open his door. "Get in, and tell me what it's all about."

Moss bent almost double to get in.

"The girl's not at home, sir. The old woman's sleeping it off, as I thought, but the daughter's gone. A chap next door said that he saw a strange man come for her, and she went off with him. Rachel Gully isn't one for the men, and from the description of this chap, he could have been Syd Carter."

"Red's brother?"

"Yes."

"*Information, sir.*"

"I want a general London call out for a girl named Rachel Gully, and a special watch kept on Red Carter and everyone associated with him," Gideon said. "Stand by for a description of the girl." He handed the microphone to Moss, listened while Moss gave a brief and precise description, and then said: "Have Red Carter taken to the divisional headquarters for questioning."

"*All noted, sir.*"

"I'm switching off," Gideon said, and flicked again. With almost the same movement he started the engine, and they began to move. "You'd better get to the station as soon as you can," he said, "and I'll have a word with Mr Christy." It would have been superfluous to ask if Moss really thought that the girl had seen the attack on Bray; as superfluous to wonder whether Moss had any personal interest in the Gully girl: obviously he had. "Anything else you think we could do to help?"

"Can't think of anything, sir," Moss answered. "But I hope that girl's all right."

"The worst they'll do is scare the wits out of her," Gideon said reassuringly.

Moss's tone altered, and he said politely: "I hope you're right, sir."

He was not reassured, but was genuinely frightened of what might happen to the girl if she had seen the attack. There was no certainty, but probably he had cause to be frightened: no one had yet proved that Red Carter's mob had killed anyone, but there had been two deaths—both officially accidental—which had never been fully explained. The trouble with Red's mob was that it had run for nearly two years without a serious set-back. Criminals with the gangster mentality always became over-confident, always began to think that they could get away with murder.

Gideon pulled up outside the ugly red-brick building which housed the NE Division's headquarters, found himself wondering when they would get round to building a new station here, and nodded good-bye to Moss, who got out and ran up the stone steps. Moss was really alarmed, and somehow managed to pass on his disquiet.

But the Gully girl couldn't be far away; she was almost certainly within half a mile of this spot, now.

"I hope to God she's all right," Gideon said to himself, and then got out to go and have a word with Christy. As he reached the top step, a car turned the corner and, moving too fast, approached the station. The driver jammed on his brakes, two doors opened almost simultaneously, and Gideon had a sense of foreboding that this was bad news.

Instead, he saw that the first man to get out was handcuffed to another; the first man was a divisional detective sergeant, named Willis, and the man handcuffed to him was small, round-faced and bald-headed.

"Baldy!" Gideon found himself exclaiming.

The sergeant was grinning, obviously on top of the world; the other man who got out of the police car raised his hands together like a boxer acknowledging the crowd. The policeman on duty at the foot of the steps was making a desperate attempt in dumbshow to tell the newcomers that Gideon was here, but they did not take the hint: and Gideon could not blame them, for Baldy Lock had been on the wanted list for nine months. He had got away with fifteen thousand pounds in a pay snatch, and no one on the Force had seen him since.

Then all three men coming up the steps saw Gideon. Willis missed a step, Baldy Lock looked downwards, as if he did not want to meet Gideon's eye, and a plainclothes man with them announced:

"We've caught Baldy Lock, sir," and then flushed as he realised the inanity of the comment.

"We'll have to mention you two in dispatches," Gideon said. "Where'd you get him?"

"Followed his wife, sir—she led the way to an old barge in Duck's Pool. He's just back from Holland, judging from some money in his pocket and some papers."

"Fine. Didn't see Syd or Red Carter on the way, did you?"

"Well, as a matter of fact," Willis said, quite casually, "I did see Syd Carter. He had a girl with him. Going towards Duck's Pool for a bit of you-know-what, I should think. Don't want him for anything, do we?"

CHAPTER 4

DUCK'S POOL

Duck's Pool was nearly half a mile from the river, a disused unloading point for barges which, years ago, had weaved their way through the small canals and the backwaters which led off the Thames. Now, with mechanical loading and unloading taking far less time, unloading stations nearer the main docks were used and Duck's Pool, like dozens of others in the vicinity, had been left to become foul and noisome. Moored alongside were five old barges, two of them little more than rotting hulls, one of them towed here only a few months after having her bows staved in. Occasionally, tramps used the barges as doss-houses; more often, the lovers of the night came out, to use the hard boards as divans. By day, especially when it was hot, children played, tossed stones at old tin cans or at sections of the barges that were not yet broken. Here, the neighbourhood's cats were drowned. Here, the occasional drunk fell in and was drowned, also. And here one of the people, whose 'accidental' death had never really been accounted for, had fallen to his death; he had been known to quarrel with Red Carter only a few days before his end.

One approach to Duck's Pool, from the south, was protected by a high warehouse wall. No one coming from that direction could be seen, and it was along here that Rachel Gully came with Syd Carter's right arm entwined in hers in such a way that she could not free herself.

It seemed an age since she had opened the front door and seen him standing there, tall, dark-haired, strong; a bigger man than his brother, whom he seemed to worship. He had piercing dark eyes and shaggy eyebrows, and he talked very little; no one expected Syd to say much.

"Want to talk to you," he had said.

"I–I can't come out now. My Mum—"

"Come on," he had insisted.

Rachel had been doing what she was told nearly all her life, and she had always been frightened of men like the Carters because her mother had thrust such fear deep into her. She had heard her mother snoring in her chair, her arms hanging by its sides. She had tried to resist when Syd had taken her arm and drawn her forward.

It was a warm evening, and she had left without a hat or coat, heart thumping painfully. She had heard Carter slam the door. He had let her go for a moment, and she had felt an awful urge to run, had been about to when he had caught her again; since then he had not let her go. She had not realised where they were heading until she had seen the warehouse wall, with its empty windows gaping against the darkening sky; she knew the reputation of Duck's Pool as well as anyone in the East End.

In panic she tried to draw back.

"Come on," he growled, and twisted her arm a little, thrusting her forward so that she walked a step ahead of him. She was finding it hard to breathe now; her asthma made the air wheeze through her lungs. She saw the oily, slimy water of the pool, sinister in the fading light. She saw the old barges. She knew that people had drowned here. She knew that Syd had not come here with her simply because she was a girl to take.

"I don't want to go along there!" She gasped.

"Want to talk to you," Syd said. "Don't want anyone to hear, neether." They neared the pool itself, and the uneven cobbles were slippery. Once Rachel slipped. "Step lively," Syd ordered, and thrust her towards two planks which stretched over a yard of water between the side of a boat and the cobbles.

She wanted to scream but could not make a sound.

She stepped on to the planks, and there was an awful fear in her lest he should push her into the water; but he held her steady. They stepped on to the creaking boards of the barge, and then stopped at the entrance to the living quarters. It was like the opening of a dark hole.

"Get down there," Syd ordered.

"Syd, no, I—"

He gave her a shove, and she fell forward, snatched at a hand rail, and jolted it out of its socket. She nearly pitched into the hole, but somehow steadied herself, and then began to climb down the upright ladder, the only means of getting in or out. There was a stench of foul water, making her feel sick. Syd filled the entrance now, and it was pitch dark in here. She heard him scramble down.

"Syd—"

"You see Tiny Bray tonight?"

"No! No, Syd, I—"

"You're lying," Syd said, and his hand touched hers, his fingers gripped her wrist and twisted. "You tell the cops anything?"

"*No!*"

"If you told the cops—"

"I tell you I didn't."

"What didn't you tell them?" he demanded, and the pressure of his fingers became more painful.

"They wanted to know if I'd seen anyone in the Cut, but they didn't make me say anything. I didn't say a word, Syd, I swear it."

"Did you see Tiny in the Cut?"

"I–yes, I did, but I didn't tell the police."

"See anyone else?"

"*No!*"

"Why don't you tell the truth?" Syd demanded roughly. Every question he asked came tautly, as if he disliked the need for saying so much; and with every question there was a little extra pressure and pain. "Who did you see set on Bray?"

"I–I didn't mean to see anyone, Syd. I didn't stay, I just went round the long way."

"See Red?" Syd demanded.

"Yes, I did see him, I happened to see him," Rachel almost sobbed, "but I didn't say anything to the police, and I never will, I swear I never will."

"That's right, you won't," Syd said. "Okay, you can get out, now. I'll give you a hand up."

The change in his mood was almost as frightening as if he had struck her, or kept calling her a liar. He hauled himself out of the stinking little hutch, and then stretched down for her. He took her wrists, tightened his grip, and hauled her up bodily. Her knees scraped against the boards. Then, in the darkness which now seemed complete, he held her with his left arm round her waist, and they went towards the side.

She *knew* what he was going to do.

She kicked out at him, and the sharp toe of her shoe caught his ankle. He gasped. She pulled herself free, and tried to run towards the boards which spanned the gap between the barge and the bank. In a moment, he was after her. She heard him swear. She was still free, and could just make out the bank; but she was too far from the boards, and the only hope for her was to jump. She ran three paces, and then leapt—but before she actually left the ground, her feet were hooked from under her; so instead of jumping clear, she pitched forward. She saw stars and the pale light reflected on the water as it seemed to come up to meet her.

She screamed.

She heard sounds, not knowing what they were, except that there seemed to be a great roaring in her ears as she met the water.

* * * * *

It was a uniformed man, whose beat included Duck's Pool and who picked up the alarm from a police call-box, who reached the pool and saw Rachel plunge into the water. He saw the man, too, and knew that the man had pushed her in, but he decided quickly to try to save the girl and to let the man go. He stripped off his tunic and helmet, and dived in. As he did so, lights shone from the two lanes which led to the pool, and he knew that the first car-load of police had arrived. He went under the noisome water, came up, saw lights flashing on the surface, and one beam falling on the hair of the girl. He was near enough to grab her, and to keep her afloat until ropes were flung for him to grip. He heard shouting and thought he heard running footsteps, but his only worry was to keep the girl's head above water.

*   *   *   *   *

"She all right?" asked Gideon.

"She will be. Frightened stiff at the moment."

"Get a doctor for her."

"One's on the way."

"Good. Got the man?"

"Yes. It was Syd Carter," answered the detective inspector who had arrived with the first police car. "He won't say much, but we can pick up Red and the rest of the bunch now. Bit of luck, that was. If Willis hadn't noticed Syd Carter and the girl, we wouldn't have found her until we'd dragged half the pools in the district."

It was part of that untidy pattern of London life; Baldy Lock, out of the country for nearly a year, had been caught when everyone had thought that he had got away for good. Baldy had come to see his wife—and because of his love for her this girl had been saved, and Syd Carter caught almost before the hunt had started. The girl owed her life to young Moss, of course, and Moss's powers of observation weren't luck.

Gideon waited until the local police surgeon had come, confirmed that all the girl needed was rest, made sure that Christy would have her looked after, and then drove homewards. He called the Yard on the radio; nothing outstanding had happened, there was no need for him to go there. He drove home along the Embankment, feeling relaxed and relieved. It was always good when a hunt ended so quickly, and it was easy to forget how many did.

But the Borgman hunt was not likely to end quickly, even if it really began.

Was Kate right after all? Was he really wise to stick his neck out? Would he ever be able to find out why Nurse Kennett had left the country, and whom she had married—whether she had married at all. It might mean giving work to a dozen police forces, in England and abroad, all of them already heavily overworked. Even if a lot of morphine was found in the first Mrs Borgman's grave, could he stand up in court on the evidence so far available, and be cross-examined by Percy Richmond?

Could he even be sure that Borgman was guilty?

He reached home, took the car to the garage just round the corner—it was a small garage, too narrow for backing in; even backing out in the mornings had its problems—and strolled in the pleasant evening to the house. No lights were on. It wasn't yet ten o'clock, Kate wouldn't be back until nearly eleven, and the youngsters might be even later. It was hard to realise that they were all sufficiently grown up to be their own judges of the right time to get home. None of them overstepped the freedom which he and Kate gave them. Now there was luck: in their children.

He and Kate had six in all, although they had lost one, very young. Tom was twenty-eight, married and an electrical research worker in the north. Prudence, at twenty-three, was married, too, but her Peter was proud that she was still a violinist with the B.B.C. Symphony Orchestra. Plump, pretty Penelope was nearly seventeen, a promising pianist who would probably soon have to choose between marriage and a career. And there was Priscilla, the quiet one, soon to be twenty-one, without a boy-friend or any special bent, but in an almost guilty way Gideon had a particularly soft spot for her.

There was Matthew, determined to be a policeman yet studying hard for his university scholarship, and young Malcolm, the 'baby', a boisterous fifteen, who gave no thought to anything but cricket, swimming, football and food.

Yes, Gideon had a lot of cause for domestic satisfaction, and nearly everything was going well at the Yard, too. For once, it looked as if the police were pegging crime down: preventative methods were beginning to work. There had been some slight increase in the uniformed branch's strength, which helped, and four out of five of the worst crooks were inside; unless a new bunch grew up in the next year or two, organised and professional crime was likely to be subdued perhaps for as long as five years—

until the men now in jail began to come out. There would be the amateurs, the big and the little Borgmans, the wife murderers, the poisoners, the embezzlers, the hundreds and the thousands of people who became criminals more by accident of events than by intent.

Which was true of Borgman?

What should he do about this *bête noire* of his? The easiest thing would be to say to the Assistant Commissioner and Plumley, of the Legal Department, that he had come to the conclusion that there was insufficient evidence to justify an exhumation. They would shake their heads and say how sorry they were but they would be relieved, for all senior officials dreaded the possibility of the failure of a big prosecution.

This might be the last chance of getting Borgman, though, and it remained a fact that if he got away with one wife murder, he might try another. His second wife was very wealthy in her own right.

Kate came in first, bright-eyed, rested after enjoying the film, but wise enough not to say too much about it. Then Matthew arrived, dark-haired, big and bony, whistling the kind of tune that made Gideon suspect that there was a girl on his mind; and within minutes plump, fair-haired, merry-eyed Penny arrived. They crowded into the kitchen-dining-room, eating sandwiches, drinking coffee, talking about a dozen things but not once mentioning crime.

Gideon gave crime hardly a thought when he got into bed beside Kate.

* * * * *

That was about the time that Borgman was kissing his wife and saying how sorry he was that he had been kept so late at a dinner with an American agent; and then because it was on the top of his mind, he told Charlotte about the discovery that Ben Samuel had been swindling him.

"What a nuisance, dear," Charlotte said absently.

Borgman thought, with clinical detachment:

'I wonder if I would have married her if I'd known what a witless fool she was?'

CHAPTER 5

ARGUMENT

ROGERSON, THE Assistant Commissioner, had been on sick leave for nearly seven months, and back in the office for two; he was looking bronzed and well, thinner than before the leave, and perhaps a little less inclined to leave everything to Gideon, who had acted as his deputy during those seven months, as well as handling his own job. Rogerson was a brisk, pleasant, friendly type; a good-natured man, a little self-conscious because he had been away so long. Plumley, of the Yard's Legal Department and the chief liaison with the Public Prosecutor's Office, was an elderly man who knew practically every trick in the prosecution's locker, and was an expert at picking out the flaws in a case; his motto was: "*When in doubt let them get away with it.*" He would put this into words, smiling as he did so, for he was an affable man whose geniality often concealed excessive caution.

They met in the Assistant Commissioner's office, just along the passage from Gideon's, at ten o'clock.

"Well, George," Rogerson said, "I'll bet you a pound I know what you're going to recommend."

"So will I," said Plumley.

"Like me to write it on a piece of paper, and put it in a hat?" Gideon asked easily. "What's your view, A.C.?"

"I'm open to persuasion."

"More than I am," said Plumley. "George, only a lunatic would go ahead against Borgman on the strength of this." He rested a pink, well-manicured hand on a file of papers nearly two inches thick. "I've had everything checked and re-checked. If we could go to that Nurse Kennett, get a signed statement from her, and make sure we could put her in the box, I might be inclined to take a chance. But—"

"Never known you take a chance yet," Gideon rejoined.

"Forgotten Fred Lee? Forgotten the Ditchburn case? We got two adverse verdicts, George."

"Nothing to do with taking chances," Gideon retorted. "You didn't prepare the cases properly."

"No use trying to needle me," Plumley said, and looked as if he even relished the thrust. "A.C., don't listen to him. He wants to go ahead with it regardless. I see from Appleby's report—and he's as shrewd a Yard lawyer as we've got—that he agrees with me. Borgman would get Richmond, and Richmond would tear this case to shreds. It wouldn't get past the police court."

Gideon said mildly: "I've been about myself quite a bit, Plum."

"We can all make mistakes."

"That's what I'm anxious about," Gideon said. He felt as if he were arguing with one of his sons, when they were just beginning to feel old enough to differ from him; it did not exasperate him, but made him feel stubborn and set on his purpose. Plumley was equally set against the Borgman case and the more they argued the broader his smile would become, the nicer his tone, and the stiffer his opposition: at times he would become positively childish. Rogerson was really an unknown quantity; but if he said no, then Borgman could be forgotten unless new evidence was obtained, and Gideon had regained the feeling of urgency which he could not properly explain. "All this talk about not having a chance doesn't ring a bell with me," he went on. "We would have to prove murder, and could work two ways. In the first place there's the accident, so-called, and—"

"But that old woman said she was poisoned."

"The death certificate says that she died as a result of multiple injuries following a car accident," said Gideon. "So that's where we would start. We've some evidence that the brakes of her car had been tampered with; we know that a good lawyer could say that this was not with malicious intent, and that Borgman actually tried to improve the holding power of the brakes. The point we would need to prove was that he did tamper with them. If we can—"

"Steady, George," Plumley's smile was very bright. "In the first place, how can we prove he himself touched the brakes? And in the second place, how could we prove malicious intent or intent to murder? That's the weakness all along; there are too many ways in which Borgman can wriggle out."

"Mind listening for a minute?" asked Gideon, with a deliberate touch of asperity. "We checked his garage and the chauffeur-gardener he used to employ, and they swore they hadn't adjusted the brakes, but expert witnesses said they had been adjusted."

"The same witness said there was a flaw in the metal of the brake-drums," Plumley interpolated.

"The point is, the brakes had been tampered with, and Borgman was pushed for money at the time. We won't have any trouble in proving that. Then we have the fact that his wife was wealthy and the fact that she was three months gone. We know from the terms of her own inheritance that a large proportion of her money would have to go to her child or her children. We can show that if a child had been born, Borgman wouldn't have been able to get anything like so much of her money. As it was, he got nearly half a million, the foundation of his fortune. There's motive enough, and there's the reason for the timing of the attempt."

"It could look good in a police court, I suppose," Plumley said, grudgingly. "But once Richmond got on the job at the Assizes—"

"Plum, there are times when I wonder if you think you're talking to a lot of first-year recruits," said Gideon heavily. "If ever there's a job on which we'd have to use our big guns in the police court, this is it. We can only pull our surprises there; at the Assizes we'd be hamstrung. We need a definite plan of campaign—say, get the usual remand in custody at the first hearing, and be ready to put all our cards on the table at the second hearing, when they'd expect us to ask for another remand.

Borgman will have to get Richmond in early to try to save himself from being sent for trial, anyhow. See what I mean?"

"You'd stand or fall on the police court hearing, would you?" Plumley was thoughtful.

"Yes. We'd work up the case on the accident, and have Richmond pulling out all the stops to demolish it. We'd say the brakes were fixed so as to cause an accident, although the motive is our weakness and Borgman's strength. I think—we all think—that Borgman found the manufacturing flaw, made it worse, and was able to sit back and let the coroner blame the manufacturer. We'll spend a lot of time on elaborating that, but won't be able to prove it, and nearly everything we build up, Richmond will mow down."

"I won't deny that," interpolated Plumley.

"When he's made us look fools and put all the doubt he wants to in the mind of the magistrate, we'll come up with the morphine angle," Gideon went on equably. "We'll do a hush-hush exhumation, get a secret report, put Bolting up. Bolting's just the right pathologist to feed Richmond with when he thinks the case is going his way. We'll try to get that nurse back in time, but if we can't we'll work in the old woman's statement, which—"

"It would never be admitted," Plumley snapped.

"We can bring it out when asking the doctor, who'll testify whether he knew this nurse. I've told you we know we haven't got a cut and dried case, so we've got to worry Borgman," Gideon insisted. "This will worry him badly. We want—"

"We don't even *know* there will be a lot of morphine in the remains, but everyone knows there'll be some," Plumley argued. There was evidence of strain behind his smile. "I don't want to appear unreasonable, George, and I agree that if we could get the Public Prosecutor to adopt these rather dubious tactics—"

Gideon broke in angrily: "What the hell do you mean—dubious tactics? What's the matter with you?—the man's a killer, he may kill again, he's in the right position for it.

We want to get a committal for trial and a conviction—and we won't get it by pussyfooting along as if we were scared of a Queen's Counsellor. What's the matter with you? Even if we lose the verdict and Borgman gets away with it, his present wife will be warned what to expect and he would never dare to try it again. That's the worst that can come out of it. And you talk about dubious tactics because I want to get a guilty verdict on a murderer! If that's the way you propose to advise the P.P.'s office, I might as well throw my hand in. I thought our job was to prevent crime as much as catch criminals."

Plumley had stopped smiling.

Rogerson's face was straight, but there was a twinkle in his eyes as he looked at Gideon, while Plumley stared down his plump nose.

After a long pause, Plumley said: "Well, if we do go ahead and come a cropper, don't say I didn't warn you. I won't oppose an exhumation order, if that's what you're really after for a start."

"If there's not much morphine we can forget it," said Rogerson. "If there is, we'll advise the P.P. to go ahead. Agreed, Plum?"

"Under protest," Plumley said. "Where is she buried?" He actually seemed to brighten up. "Or was she cremated? If Borgman really poisoned her, you'd think—"

"Her will directed that she should be buried," Gideon said. "She's out at Maidenhead. Borgman's flying to Paris tomorrow, and we can get everything done and the result known before he's back. If we find nothing he can protest if he wants to, if we find what I expect to find it won't matter what he does."

"Well, that's all the time we need spend on that," said Rogerson, as if with relief. "Now there's the Tiny Bray murder. You've got Syd Carter up this morning on a charge of attempted murder of the girl Gully, haven't you?"

"Over in NE Court, yes," said Gideon. "His brother will be in the same court, charged with the murder of Tiny Bray. There's no problem. We need a formal eight-day remand, then we can put up some of the evidence and have them both committed. Right, Plum?"

"For once I agree with you," Plumley said.

He was smiling, if a little tautly, when the conference broke up, just after eleven o'clock.

* * * * *

That was the time when Ben Samuel was standing in Borgman's office, white-faced, staring at Borgman as he lifted the telephone and said:

"Get me Scotland Yard at once—the Criminal Investigation Department."

* * * * *

It was Gideon's custom to go through all the cases being handled by his Department at least once a day, and to discuss the next move with the officers in charge, and, as often as not, with the Divisions. On conference mornings there was no time to do this, and he liked to leave it until the afternoon, although it was not so satisfactory, as many of the men whom he wanted to talk to would be out on the job. That morning, he made notes about what to do once the result of the exhumation was known, laid everything on with the Berkshire police, who would visit the cemetery after dark tonight, but keep the exhumation as quiet as they could. With great deliberation, trying to make sure that every step was absolutely sound, he prepared the opening stages of the case against John Borgman. Occasionally, an uneasy thought obtruded: what would he feel if Plumley were proved right, and there were not sufficient traces of morphia? But there was no need to dwell on that.

Remembering Kate's upbraiding the night before, he went to lunch at a nearby pub, and returned to the office at a little after two o'clock. Chief Inspector Bell was now his chief *aide*, an elderly man by the Department's standards, in the middle fifties. He was a quiet, good-humoured old trooper who knew almost as much about each job as Gideon, but who always lacked Gideon's subconscious aggressiveness and sense of purpose. He looked sticky and warm as he sat at a small desk opposite

Gideon's, the sun striking a corner of the window, and rippling on the river which was only a stone's throw from the room.

"Hallo, Joe," Gideon said.

"Had a nice nap, George?"

"Don't you start," said Gideon, and took off his coat, hooked it on to the back of his chair, loosened his collar, and picked up a thick file of reports "Was that furrier raided?"

"No. Looks as if the Carters were planning that job."

"I've asked Christy to dig; he'll find out. Anything fresh in about Rachel Gully?"

"She'll have a week on the sick list."

"Staying home?"

"No—staying with some friends. Friends of a copper named Moss, if you ask me."

"Wouldn't be surprised. Any news from Australia?"

"Not a word."

"Bound to be, soon," Gideon said.

"Unless Borgman had the nurse bumped off," Bell said, and grinned.

"You're worse than Plumley."

"I had a word with Ellis, and he says Plumley got back to the office profaning the sacred name of Gideon."

"I can believe it. How'd that case go in Horsham?"

"The old man was committed for trial."

"How can seventy play around with seven?" Gideon asked himself, and was sorting through the reports in front of him, marking with a pencil those he would want to return to. "Fred Lee in?"

"Yes. Know what I'd do, if I were you?"

"What?"

"Give Fred a couple of months' sick leave."

"Not on your life. He'd apply for his pension before it was over," Gideon said. "Know what I'm going to do?"

"I've got a nasty idea. You're going to put Fred Lee on to the Borgman job, because this will bring him up against Richmond again."

"That's right."

The Chief Inspector said: "George, I know what's on your mind: you think if Fred can be on the winning side against Richmond, it will put him right on top of himself again. Don't forget the other possibility, will you? It might finish him off."

Gideon said, very slowly: "He's finishing himself off as he's going now, and if he went quickly after another shouting match with Richmond, it would be kinder."

"I hope you're right," Bell said. Then he gave his friendly and rather tired smile, and eased his damp, crumpled collar. "You usually are, I suppose. Tell you what came in just now—I haven't put it on paper yet: that Robson woman's husband turned up."

"Okay?"

"Under two feet of garden soil."

Gideon jerked up his head. "That a fact?"

"Would I pull your leg? In the garden of an empty house round the corner from his home. I've been talking to Ragg at HI. He says there's been talk that Mrs Robson has a boy friend, and that's why she didn't trouble to report her missing hubby. If his employers hadn't forced the issue we probably wouldn't have known about it. Ragg's digging."

"What kind of hole?"

"When I said two feet, I meant it."

"Remember what the soil's like out at HI?" asked Gideon.

"Heavy clay, according to the report."

"Good thick clay, I know that spot," said Gideon. "And the description of Mrs Robson is that she's about five feet three, and small."

"All right, all right," said Bell. "She probably didn't dig her husband's grave. George, did I ever tell you that I marvel at you?"

"Forget it," said Gideon, and marked another report, then glanced down at the one beneath it. He was aware that Joe Bell was behaving as if nursing some secret he found difficult to keep to himself; now he glanced up and saw the other man grinning. He looked down at the report again. It was in Bell's writing, and there was no doubt that it had been slipped into the middle of the pile so as to make sure that he did not see it at once. Bell had been able to savour the waiting period, getting a silent laugh every time he, Gideon, had turned over a report. To rob the other of his triumph, Gideon kept an absolutely straight face, but his heart was racing.

This was a report from the Information Room about a request from Borgman Enterprises Limited to investigate irregularities in a cashier's accounts: an invitation from John Borgman to make free in one part of his businesses.

Gideon looked up, and gave an expansive grin. Bell started to chuckle.

"A little bit of what you fancy does you good," he said. "I told Appleby to go over and stall a bit, just to size up the situation, and he's probably there still. It looks as if an old chap has been diddling them for years. Don't know very much about it yet, but it means we're right inside the sanctum sanctorum, so to speak, on Borgman's invitation. If he knew what you've been cooking up he'd have a shock."

"I'm wondering whether I ought to have the shock," said Gideon. His thoughts had flown to the absent nurse. If Borgman had any reason to fear the police, would he invoke the Yard on a comparatively small matter?

"Now what?" Bell asked.

"Would he send for us if—" Gideon began, and then shrugged his shoulders.

"His first wife died nearly five years ago, and he's probably almost forgotten her already," Bell said. "If you're right about Borgman, he doesn't look backwards."

Gideon spread his hands.

"It'll give Appleby a chance to size him up, and soon I'll send Fred over. Between them, they're not likely to be far wrong in their judgment. If I'm not here when Appleby comes, send round for me—I won't be out of the building."

"Can't wait for it, eh, George?"

"That's right," said Gideon.

"I suppose you're right about Fred?"

"I've been waiting the chance to try him out for a long time," Gideon said, "and this is just his kind of job. If anything is going to get him back on form, it's his memory for details, and he was in the early inquiries into Mrs Borgman's death. I know he doesn't trust his memory so much since Richmond proved that he'd slipped up once, but I trust it."

"O.K., George," Bell said.

They did not have to wait long for news about Borgman. After Gideon had seen three of the officers in charge of current investigations and had talked to HI about the murder of the man Robson, there was a perfunctory tap, and the door was thrust open. It was Appleby. Appleby, when tired and jaded, looked an old man, every day of his sixty-four. Appleby when something had gone right was a sprightly fifty, and now he was at his brightest. There was a glow at his cheeks, and he raised his hand to Gideon in a mock salute.

"George," he announced, "I think you're right."

"Quick change, Jim." Gideon hid his fresh misgivings.

"First time I've ever been face to face with Borgman and I wouldn't trust him as far as I would Red Carter. That man goes deep and nasty."

"Think so?"

"I know so. I've only met two or three of them in my natural, and you can take it from me Borgman won't let anything get in his way. I don't say you won't be a fool to have a shot at him, but having met him—boy, oh boy, would I like to see him in dock."

"I know what you mean," Gideon remarked dryly.

"There's the poor devil of a cashier," went on Appleby, and in brisk sentences explained what had happened. "I don't know the background, and fraud's fraud, but the old man looked as if he could die on the spot. Borgman talked to him as if he were a louse. He talked to me," added Appleby cautiously, "as if I were a dog. I've met that ash-blonde secretary—she has the longest, shapeliest legs you ever saw, too. I think I would start checking on her, and the situation between Borgman and his present wife."

"You ought to know Gee-Gee by now," said Bell. "Always something up his sleeve."

"What have you done so far, Jim?" asked Gideon.

"Taken the details—looks as if the fraud goes back about thirteen years—and told Borgman that we would be in touch with him. He seemed to think that I ought to clap the darbies on old Samuel right away, and when he found I wasn't going to, he sent the old man packing without even a chance to take his personal belongings from his desk. There isn't much doubt about the fraud—Samuel admitted it, anyhow—but Borgman doesn't seem to think we need to check anything. He barks 'Arrest that man!' so we ought to jump to it. He's the original pocket dictator, George, but—"

"Don't spoil it," urged Bell.

"I would like to take him on myself," said Appleby reflectively. "He's as crafty and clever as he's deep. Don't know when it was I was last impressed so much by a man's potential." Appleby rubbed his hands together, and then finished: "I'd like to see you come head on with him though, Gee-Gee! What happened at the conference today?"

"If there's a lot of morphine at the autopsy, we go right ahead."

"Last night I hoped you wouldn't find boracic powder," Appleby said, "but today—you heard me first time. Mind if I stick my big nose in?"

"Not in your present mood."

"Well, this is the kind of job Fred Lee would be good at," said Appleby, almost diffidently. "You know how it is with Fred. He's happier with columns of figures and pounds shillings and pence than I am with my fork and spade, and that's saying something. When he's studied accounts he remembers all the details, too. You could send him over to the Borgman empire and let him take root for a few days. Fred would be just the man to keep thinking up awkward little queries, and telling Borgy that as he's called us in, we have to make a job of it. And the longer Fred was there the more he'd find out about Borgman and the blonde. Also," Appleby went on, rather doggedly, because he had won no response, "if we got Borgman, and Fred had a finger in the pie, it might pull him round." He stopped, scowled, and demanded gruffly: "What's the matter now? Since when has Fred Lee's name been poison?"

"It's just that we're bored," Bell said. "George decided to send Fred there five minutes after he heard about this. Now you know why you were never a commander."

"Good old Gee-Gee," Appleby brayed.

Gideon was shifting his chair back.

"We'll see about that later. About this old man, Samuel, Jim. Did you say he looked all in?"

"One foot in the grave already."

"And sent packing?"

"Minute's notice."

"Got his address?"

"Yes, and you're not the only one who can see further than his nose. I sent a chap after him, too. Don't want him to throw himself under a bus before we can get to work on his boss, do we?" Appleby was looking very self-satisfied. "I've asked the Division to check on Samuel and his family, and asked for a report before you go home tonight; we should be able to get a good picture of the situation. I know one thing: Samuel's down as far as a chap can go, and Borgman enjoyed kicking him."

Gideon didn't speak.

"You want to know something?" Appleby asked, in a marvelling tone. "It was only this afternoon that I saw anything funny about the name of Borgman's yacht. Funny peculiar, I mean. You seen it?"

Bell said: "The *Lucretia*."

"Lucretia Borgia, the famous Italian poisoning family," Appleby hammered home his point. "You seen that before, George?"

"Yes," Gideon said, and remembered how the name had affected him when he had first suspected that Borgman had poisoned his wife, and wondered whether a man with a name like *Borg*man could be so brazen as to christen a ship like that. But the yacht, nine years old, had been named before Borgman had bought it, and there was a superstition against changing the name of boats. "Tell me more about this blonde, Jim."

"Very cool and poised, very efficient, very nice, very bedworthy. If I were you, I'd have Fred find out what the staff at the Borgman Empire think about her."

"I'll lay it on," Gideon said. "Put all this down on paper, Jim, will you?"

"Yep."

"And ask Fred to come in."

"Okay," Appleby said, and went out, letting the door close itself on his heels.

Almost immediately afterwards, a messenger brought in a sealed envelope. Gideon opened this at once and had a moment of triumph: this was the exhumation order for Borgman's first wife. He was about to tell Bell, when a telephone rang on Bell's desk. As he lifted it, Gideon's nearest telephone rang, and he picked it up; and, almost at once, an inter-office telephone rang. He said: "Hold on," into the first mouthpiece, and "Gideon," into the second. It was Rogerson, who said:

"Can you come and see me right away, George?"

"I'd rather have ten minutes."

"Make it as soon as you can."

"Right," Gideon promised, and put one receiver down and picked up the other. "Gideon . . . What's that, Hugh? . . ." He began to smile, and Bell, putting his receiver down, glanced across as if puzzled. "Fine," he said. "Got 'em just where we want 'em. Wonder how Tiny got hold of it? . . . Yes, I know we're going to miss Tiny." He replaced the receiver and called across to Bell: "There was a plan of the furriers in Red Carter's wallet; no doubt he was going to lay on that job. You got anything new?"

"Three cars stolen from Piccadilly this lunch hour."

"Bet they weren't locked," Gideon said. "What do

motorists think keys are for? How many is that from the West End this week?"

"Twenty-nine in the West End, a hundred and four in our whole area."

Gideon pursed his lips. "Looks more than ever as if it's organised. We'll have a couple of dummy cars laid on and watched: better check the actual places where most of the thefts are from, first." He got up and went to a small map of Central London which was hanging on the wall, and Bell came across. "Can you mark 'em?" Bell picked up some red-headed pins and stuck them in. "Makes a pattern," Gideon mused. "See how near a corner each job has been—all from short streets, all one-way streets to make fairly sure the way couldn't be blocked . . . lay on a special watch at all corners, will you?"

"Right."

"And we'll go down and have a look at the big map," Gideon said. "Might be worth more thought than we've given to it. I've got—" A telephone rang on his desk, and he gave a lugubrious kind of grin. "Looks as if things are really waking up." He turned round and picked up the receiver. "Gideon . . . *What?* . . . Oh, God."

The tone of his voice was so bleak that Bell stood watching and waiting anxiously. He knew how keenly Gideon felt about so much that happened; how readily he took the responsibility for things which went wrong although other people had caused the trouble. The curious thing about Gideon was a kind of sensitiveness which would have made many people bad policemen, but made him exceptional. "Tell you what," he said, decisively, "ask Borgman to come here to see me. . . . No, he doesn't have to, but it would be worth trying." He held on for a moment, then said: "All right, Jim." He rang off, looked silently at Bell for some minutes, and then said: "The cashier Samuel killed himself and his invalid wife as soon as he got home today."

CHAPTER 6

KILLER CAR

FOR A few moments Gideon sat quite still and silent. He had never seen Samuel and knew little about him, but a weight of gloom lay heavy upon him when Bell asked:

"How did he do it?"

"Cyanide from a weed-killer."

"So Jim didn't watch 'em closely enough," Bell said.

"Ought to have brought him here," Gideon growled. "I was a bit afraid of it. The first few hours are always the most dangerous." He did not add that he knew that Appleby had not brought Samuel here for questioning because Borgman had expected him to; Appleby's dislike of Borgman would cut both ways.

"Think Borgman will come here?" Bell wondered.

"It's anyone's guess," Gideon said, and was in no mood to tell Bell that he had the exhumation order.

His telephone bell rang.

"I'll answer it," Bell said, and came across, while Gideon went to the door and waited, looking round; he was never easy in his mind at walking out on a telephone call. He saw Bell's expression harden, saw the quick glance which seemed to say: 'Don't go,' and went back to the desk. "Hold on," said Bell, put a hand over the mouthpiece, and said: "Another car theft from the West End. One of our chaps saw it, and blew his whistle. The thief drove on to the pavement to get away, and knocked down a youngster."

"Hurt badly?"

"Dead."

"Get our chap's description of the driver out as fast as you can make it," Gideon ordered. "I'll be in the Map Room in half an hour." He went out, his jaw clamped, angry at this senseless death, angry at the viciousness which could make a car thief take such a wild chance. 'A youngster'; and behind the youngster, a mother, father, girl friends, brothers, sisters—the aftermath of death, which was often grief, and sometimes despair. The car thefts from the West End had been nagging him for weeks; he should have given them more attention.

He tapped cursorily on the door marked *Assistant Commissioner* and went in. Rogerson was alone at his desk, writing. He glanced up, waved to a chair, finished what he was doing very quickly, and then pushed his chair back. His expression told Gideon that he did not like what he had to say.

"Done anything about that exhumation yet, George?"

"I've laid on the job," Gideon answered.

"I'm afraid you'll have to lay it off," said Rogerson.

Gideon checked a question, and sat there solidly, his face expressionless, thought of the death of the youngster pushed aside. It was remarkable how often thought of Borgman did push everything else into the background.

"Don't you want to know why?" asked Rogerson.

"Don't I know?"

"It wasn't Plumley."

"If Plumley agreed to work on the result of the exhumation he wouldn't back out. Someone high-up doesn't want to risk a smack-down."

"That's right."

"Who?"

"Don't ask me where it started," said Rogerson. "I suspect the Home Secretary had second thoughts after he'd signed that order, but it would be worth a kick in the pants to say so. The Commissioner's non-committal, but he says that the Home Office doesn't want to delve into a case four or five years old, when it's so speculative, in view of public unrest about the present rate of crime." Rogerson was speaking with great deliberation, and badly: at heart he was angry. Gideon was beginning to feel angry, too, as he often did when he came up against the brick wall of the High Authorities, but his was a slow anger; and already he was trying to see a way of getting round this embargo. "The official attitude is that as we are understaffed, and as we can't really cope with the crop of car thefts, housebreakings, shop lifting and general indictables, and since we can't hold back the steadily worsening crime figures, even though big stuff's on the down graph, this is no time to have several men delving back into a case which might be imaginary."

Gideon said flatly: "I've asked Borgman to come and see me today."

Rogerson actually gaped.

Gideon told him why in some detail, including the suicide and wife-murder. Rogerson nodded, made no comment, but pushed some papers across his desk and said: "I'll have a look at him while he's here. Take those papers with you, they're not so hot." Gideon saw that they were the latest Home Office statistics, and he was reasonably sure that the number of indictable offences had gone up by nearly twenty per cent over last year. He had been over-optimistic. In spite of the lull of the past few weeks because so many of the big boys were inside, there was more crime than ever. A youngster run down and killed; Tiny Bray, beaten to death; the Gully girl, all but drowned; the crop of thefts of cars and from cars, of housebreaking, of pickpocketing—there was no end to it. One of the troubles was that at the Yard one became almost to accept the inevitability of a rise in the crime figures; to accept the inevitability of failure in a battle which was being waged so bitterly.

"I'll study 'em," Gideon said. "Anything else?"

"No, George. I'm sorry about Borgman."

Gideon grunted, still making no comment, still brooding. He went into his office, and asked Bell: "Anything in from Borgman?"

"No."

"I'm going to have a look at the places where these car thefts have been from," Gideon said, picking up the exhumation order and putting it into his inside coat pocket.

He did not explain why he was going out, but Bell knew him better than most, and almost certainly realised that he was brooding over some rebuff that he wanted to ponder on his own. He had to decide what to do about that exhumation order, and he was the only one now who could make the decision. He could lift a telephone and stop the Berkshire police from proceeding—he had persuaded them to start preparing on his assurance that the order would be coming along; they wouldn't actually start to dig until they got it. If he sent it down to Berkshire, 'forgetting' to cancel it, and the body was exhumed and the autopsy finished, then he would know whether he could hope to force the hand of the men who had ordered 'no action'. He no longer felt angry, just a little sore: and that because it seemed as if Borgman, not the politicians, were to blame for this.

He entered the Map Room, where a uniformed sergeant and a plainclothes man were on duty, sticking pins in the huge maps of London which were spread out on the walls and on the stands between the walls. It was like a huge library, with bookcases at intervals so that every London Division had a big section map of its own. In each map were pins of many colours: red for fatal accidents, pink for accidents without fatalities, black for car thefts, brown for thefts from cars, grey for housebreaking . . . a colour for all the common crimes. Seen like this, it seemed as if no square inch of London was free from serious crime; and as if few spots were free from car accidents and car thefts. He hadn't been down here for a week, and he should have been, because the number of car thefts had gone up so much; he had noticed the trend, of course, and sent for special reports.

The uniformed sergeant was standing by one of the maps as Gideon walked round.

"How many car thefts reported this month, Ted?" Gideon asked. "In the whole Metropolitan police area?"

"Four hundred and thirty-one, sir."

"God! How many up on last week?"

"Seventeen."

"Week before?"

"Nineteen, sir."

"How many found?"

"One in every two, sir, usually stripped of everything that can be moved. Some are used for joy-riding, of course, quite a few for thefts and smash-and-grab jobs."

"Yes. What's the proportion of central and outer districts?"

"One in every four's inside the square mile," the sergeant said, and meant the very heart of London's West End.

"Any special trends?" asked Gideon.

"Well, I dunno, sir." The sergeant looked at the brown-headed pins, and then picked up his note-books. "I haven't noticed anything, but have a look for yourself."

"Thanks," said Gideon, and studied the figures. "Shouldn't think you'd missed anything," he went on, and picked up a telephone from the sergeant's desk, and called Information. When the chief inspector then in charge answered, he said in an even voice: "Gideon here . . . I want up-to-the-minute statistics on car thefts over the whole Metropolitan and City area—comparative figures for the past twelve months, and for the past three years. Make a thorough job of it, will you?"

"Right," the chief inspector said. "You heard about the one an hour ago?"

"Yes."

"Another man died."

"Got the driver yet?"

"No."

Gideon said: "It will be in all the headlines tonight—tell the Back Room to give the newspapers everything we can on it. Tell them I'm going to have a look at the scene myself, too. Don't give them the slightest excuse for saying that we aren't taking it seriously. Say that—"

"Someone been prodding you?"

The comment annoyed Gideon, but he did not show it. Instead, he said: "No. I'm prodding you," and rang off without finishing what he had intended to say. He nodded to the sergeant and went out of the brightly lighted room and up the stairs towards the main hall, nodding to everyone who passed and spoke or raised a hand to him. The second fatality made this a case which was going to be sensational, and now his mind was almost free from the Borgman uncertainty; he had to present the Yard in the best light he could, and try to make sure that no newspaper would start one of the periodic 'pep-up-the-Yard' campaigns.

If he had his own way he would have walked, but he did not want to be out of the office for too long, so he crossed Parliament Street, and then took a bus which dropped him at Piccadilly Circus. During the slow ride, he tried to set the Borgman business in its proper perspective. Was it really conceivable that if Borgman knew about the danger from the nurse's belated statement he would have acted so high-handedly with Appleby? Appleby had described a man who was absolutely sure of himself.

Was it a mistake to keep at Borgman 'on principle'?—because the man obsessed him? God knew that there was plenty doing to keep the Yard busy. That wasn't the point, he told himself, almost portentously; the point was that no one who had committed a crime must ever feel free from the possibility of being found out; and a five-year-old crime could have far worse repercussions on the mind of a criminal than one that had happened four or five minutes ago. He could not see himself arguing that point with the politicians, and told himself that obviously there had been some talk in the lobbies of the House of Commons. Whenever a directive came from the Home Secretary it was because he was being pushed—and probably a lot of Members of Parliament were restive about the increasing incidence of crime.

Gideon got off the bus, and said: "Damned fool." Of course, the Home Office had seen the latest figures before he had.

He walked along Shaftesbury Avenue. There was a crowd of people at one corner, being moved on by several policemen, some of whom were obviously out of patience because of the crowd's insistence. Gideon was tall enough to look over the heads of most people present. He saw a squad of his own men busy, measuring, marking the roadway and the pavement. The ambulances had gone, but the grisly tale of what had happened remained; there were patches of sawdust, some of them showing the damp of blood; and there were two small pools of blood which someone had missed; on one there was the imprint of a foot. A plate glass window had been smashed, and the killer car had been nosed inside the shop, one wing badly crumpled but otherwise hardly damaged. It was a Morris, the kind of medium-powered car easiest to steal and get away with.

Police were trying to keep the crowd back far enough for them to work in comfort, and three uniformed men came out of a shop doorway, carrying some boxes, to use as a temporary barricade. Gideon took all this in, and saw several Fleet Street men also taking in the scene; one of them was standing on a box and taking a photograph; another photographer was at a window on the first floor of the shop. Gideon knew that it was only a matter of time before a reporter came up and asked him questions; it was better to be questioned than to volunteer information.

The photographer on the box called out: "Commander!" in a loud voice, and Gideon turned towards him. A small man with the photographer came across and said earnestly:

"Investigating this in person, Mr Gideon?"

"Just having a look," Gideon said. "Had too many car thefts lately, and we're giving it priority."

"How long have you been doing that?"

"Two or three weeks."

"As long as that?"

"What do you think—that we like car thefts?" asked Gideon, as if irritably. "We can't do much without the co-operation of the public, you know that as well as I do. I'll bet that car wasn't locked."

"It wasn't, sir." A Yard man had come up, smaller than most, wearing a well-cut brown suit, hair brushed very neatly, and with an immaculate air about him. "I've talked to the owner. He forgot to lock it after lunch."

Gideon nodded, and went to the car. A divisional man was in it, brushing it over for fingerprints, but if this had been stolen by an expert, then the thief would have worn gloves, and there would be no hope of finding prints.

"The only thing we've got is a description of what he looked like from behind," the brown-clad man said. "One of our men saw him."

"Is he here?"

"The tall constable—yes."

Gideon went across, knowing that he had been identified by every policeman and newspaperman here, and by many of the crowd. He spent only a minute with the tall constable, enough to make the man glow, and then checked everything that had been done. Every shopkeeper and every front office was being visited, in the hope that someone had seen the face of the car thief; nearby shops, offices and restaurants were being visited in the same quest. Harrison, the brown-clad man, had missed nothing; his was a temperament that thrived on praise, and Gideon said:

"Keep it up and you'll get the chap all right."

This was 'his' London; the 'manor' which he had walked as a constable, and later as a sergeant; the district he had come to know inside out as a detective officer and a detective sergeant; and his first major job at the Yard had been that which Harrison had now. It was less that he loved the square mile than that it seemed natural for him to be here; the little shops in Soho, the delicatessens, the murky doorways, the laundries, the discreetly shrouded restaurants, the chatter in foreign languages, the streaming traffic, the noise, the bustling vitality, the quiet squares, the graceful Mayfair houses—to Gideon all this was the true heart of London. It never failed to restore his sense of balance. He could think more clearly and with less bias here than anywhere else, even in his own office and his own home. In a strange way he could be alone here, in spite of the throng who jostled as they passed.

He visited twenty-one places from which cars had been stolen in the past few weeks, and saw how cleverly the cars had been selected to give the greatest possible chance of a getaway, and he came firmly to the conclusion that many of these thefts were the work of one gang. If that were so, then almost certainly there were several nearby garages to which each stolen car could be driven, the number plate whipped off and replaced by a false one; there would be other garages, probably on the perimeter of the West End or even in the outer suburbs, where cars could be re-cellulosed and their appearance changed completely.

He was at the end of Shaftesbury Avenue when a plain-clothes man came up, a little diffidently, and said:

"Commander Gideon?"

"Yes."

"There's a message from your office, sir. It says that a Mr B. will be there at half past five."

Gideon said: "Good, thanks," and immediately his spirits rose; he realised how much he wanted to see Borgman, and how glad he was that Borgman had decided to accept the invitation. It was already nearly five o'clock: the quicker he got back the better. He waved to a taxi, and as it slowed down, he said to the plainclothes man:

"Call the office back, and ask them to have Superintendent Lee there for me in ten minutes, will you?"

"Very good, sir."

"Thanks, Osborn," Gideon said, and could see the astonishment in the man's eyes at being recognised. Gideon got into the taxi, sat back, and began to fondle the bowl of his pipe.

First Fred Lee; then Borgman; then the decision about the exhumation; and before he went home he must prepare an outline of what he wanted done about the car thefts, and have a word with Bell about the best man to put in charge.

He was almost buoyant when he strode into his office, where grey-haired, round-shouldered Fred Lee waited, on his own.

CHAPTER 7

BORGMAN

"Joe had to nip out," Lee said. "He won't be five minutes. He tells me you've got a special for me."

"And what a special," Gideon said. He rounded his desk and sat down. "Take a pew, Fred." He was a little over-hearty, and that was only partly due to his mood. Lee needed pushing; needed to feel at least for the time being that he was not really on his own, and that the strength and the confidence of Gideon and the Yard was behind him. In fact he was a person whom one success could make into a new man, and another serious failure destroy utterly, as a policeman. "Joe say what it was?"

"Borgman."

"That's right. An old cashier . . ." Gideon outlined the situation without wasting words, and saw the intentness with which Lee followed every point. This was undoubtedly the right job for Lee, who could make a column of figures live, and could read account books as another might read a simple report, and who also had the gift of making what he discovered clear to those who had no head for figures. He had followed through three big cases of income tax fraud brilliantly, and nothing had seemed likely to stop his progress at the Yard until, a year ago, he had been given the Rambaldi Case. This had been an involved case of income tax fraud in a series of companies of which Rambaldi had been the leading light—another Borgman in a way. There had been no question of the tax evasions, simply doubt as to whether Rambaldi had taken any part in them, or whether the onus had lain entirely with the parent company's secretary and accountants. Each of these men had accepted the responsibility, and denied that Rambaldi had known about the frauds. Lee had been sure—in the way that Gideon was now sure about Borgman—that Rambaldi had been the main architect, and that the other men were taking the rap because their wives and families were being well looked after and because each would come out of jail to a small fortune.

At one time it had looked as if the prosecution would win easily: until Percy Richmond had started the cross-examination of Fred Lee.

It had not been good to see a man made to look a fool. In the witness box, Lee had gradually broken down under the remorseless questioning, and two other witnesses on whom he had been relying had contradicted themselves so often under Richmond's questions that Rambaldi had been found not guilty. Only Lee and a few Yard officers believed that the acquitted man had been as guilty as either of the others.

The first break in Lee's testimony had come when he had forgotten some figures, under Richmond's cross-examination, and become momentarily confused. Then Richmond had attacked him on his greatest strength—his memory. If he could 'forget' one thing, couldn't he get others wrong? The jury had been duly persuaded that Lee's memory was unreliable, and his reasoning consequently faulty.

There had been a number of contributory factors to Lee's subsequent breakdown. For one thing, he had worked for three years without a real holiday; for another, the eldest of his three children had been stricken with polio, and was still badly crippled; and for a third, two other, lesser cases had gone sour on him. He had been given six months' sick leave, there had been talk of an early retirement, and it was because he hated the thought of retiring under a cloud that he had come back. But something had happened to him. His head for figures was the same, his shrewdness unmatched, but he found himself doubting the soundness of his own memory. In short, he had lost his confidence. Gideon had soon realised that he would not get it back until he had a big success.

". . . and of course what we really want is as much about Borgman as we can get," Gideon said. "Now that this cashier is dead, we've got a bigger reason than ever to probe. Borgman called us in, and we can go ahead and check back for years."

"Want to make him edgy?"

"Get him wondering what we're really after, yes."

"Supposing it's just a cut and dried job, which I can clear up in a couple of days?"

Gideon grinned. "Just get bogged down in it, Fred."

Lee hesitated, looking intently at the bigger man. He had rather worried grey eyes, which had lost much of their sharpness. His features were clear-cut, his nose long and pointed, like his chin. He had a curious shaped mouth, drooping at the corners but, in the old days, giving him a droll look. Now, it was anxious. He was a tall thin man, and had always been round-shouldered.

"Not taking too much of a chance, George, are you?" he asked. "I know how badly you want Borgman. If I muck this one up—"

"Won't do me any harm if I have to back down," Gideon said, "and between you and me it looks as if I'll have to. You can't do any real damage, but you might dig up enough to give me a chance to go for Borgman in a big way. I don't know of anyone else who can."

Lee smiled, more brightly.

"If I can get anything on him, I will all right. Want me to be here when he comes?"

"Yes."

"Thanks," said Lee, and then glanced at the telephone as it rang, and as the door opened to admit Bell, who had obviously washed and brushed his thin grey hair, and looked fresh and boyish.

"Gideon here," said Gideon. "Ah, yes. Bring him up, will you?"

He rang off.

"Joe, you sit at your desk as if you're minding your own business, but keep glancing at him now and again, and make a lot of notes," Gideon said. "We won't be able to do much tonight, but we might start a crack. Fred, you stand with your back to the window. Push that armchair round a bit, so that it faces the window—that's right. He can't turn the chair round if he has to look at you as well as me, and we'll find out what colour his eyes are!" He was smiling, and trying to hide his tension. He felt an unfamiliar, sick kind of excitement, almost a dread of this going wrong. It was a long, long time since he had first wanted Borgman here.

One of Gideon's telephones rang, and he lifted the receiver quickly, while he said to Lee:

"Tell the switchboard not to put any more calls through."

Into the telephone he said: "Gideon. What? . . . Oh, good." He rang off, and made a note, saying: "They've found some strands of blood-stained cotton on a splinter of glass from that Morris. Looks as if the driver wore cotton gloves, and cut himself."

He finished the note as there came a tap at the door; and a moment later Borgman came in.

He wasn't quite as tall as Gideon had expected, nor quite as broad. He was rather thickset, all the same, compact and extremely well-dressed in a dark grey suit with a narrow pin stripe, a light grey tie, light grey socks, a light grey handkerchief sticking out of his breast pocket. He wore a small pearl tie-pin, and somehow that added to the impression he made: of being very smooth.

Gideon stood up, rather clumsily.

"Evening, Mr Borgman. Good of you to come."

"Good-evening," Borgman said.

"Sit down," Gideon invited, and sounded as ill-at-ease as Borgman was sure of himself. He studied the man closely; the black hair, just a little too long, obviously because he wanted it that way; the rough-looking, olive skin; the dark brown eyes; the rather heavy features, except for the short nose and the short upper lip. He needed to shave twice a day, and the shadow of stubble on his face was very noticeable.

He frowned against the light, but there was Fred Lee, with his back to the window.

"I'm Gideon," Gideon announced, "and this is

Superintendent Lee, who will be in charge of the investigation at your office, Mr Borgman."

"I hardly see why a lengthy investigation is needed," Borgman said. He had a good voice, not too cultured or put on, but there was an edge to it. He was very wary, and gave the impression that he did not quite know why he was here. Gideon took his time studying him, still highly gratified that he had the man in front of him, still thinking far beyond the implications of this case, the nurse forgotten.

He said, almost apologetically: "We certainly don't want to cause unnecessary inconvenience, Mr Borgman, but we have to make sure that we know everything behind these defalcations."

"A man holding a position of trust has been robbing me. There are the books to prove it. Isn't that sufficient?"

"But he can no longer speak for himself," Gideon said.

"He admitted his guilt to me, he admitted it to your man, and when he killed himself and his wife, he proved it to *my* satisfaction," Borgman said coldly. "If he were alive, I would hold him up as an example, but you can't prosecute a dead man."

Gideon didn't speak.

"Unless you have found a way," Borgman said.

That was nearly a sneer, and obviously he did not like it here, and did not like the way that Gideon was appraising him, or the way Bell kept glancing up at him. The atmosphere was exactly as Gideon had wanted it from the beginning, and Borgman had helped to create it.

He looked as if he were about to speak again, when Gideon said:

"No, Mr Borgman, we haven't yet found a way of making the dead talk. I only wish we could." That came out quite flatly, and he was watching the other man intently all the time. He thought he saw a flash of annoyance in the dark eyes; it was easy to imagine that he actually saw a glint of fear. He paused again for what seemed a long time in a portentous way, and then went on: "Yes, I only wish we could; we would hear some strange stories from the dead. As it is, we can only try to make sure that the living are protected and that the guilty don't go unpunished."

Borgman said sharply: "Samuel's the only one who was guilty."

"Can you be sure, Mr Borgman?"

"Of course I'm sure."

"Yours is a very big organisation," Gideon said, as if he were picking his words with great care, "and this isn't the first occasion in which we have had to probe into the affairs of a large organisation. Two years ago Superintendent Lee was investigating the affairs of a company after a trifling defalcation had been discovered. A clerk had stolen a little under a hundred pounds, as far as we knew at first. But it proved that he was simply a catspaw, and that frauds of over a hundred thousand pounds were involved."

Borgman said, too sharply: "There is no reason to suspect anything of that kind in my organisation."

"Did you suspect Samuel?"

"I discovered what he was doing."

"I understand from Mr Appleby that the frauds have been going on for many years. Is that true?"

Borgman said off-handedly: "Yes. But it doesn't alter the fact that I discovered it."

"And we're very grateful that you did," said Gideon. "Had Samuel lived, of course, the investigation would have centred on him and it would have been comparatively easy to find out if anyone else was involved. His death makes it necessary to trace all the defalcations carefully, and to make sure that no one else was working with him. It's one thing for a man to commit suicide because he has been caught out in a crime, Mr Borgman, and quite another thing if a man has killed himself because he was driven to desperation by accomplices. We have to be absolutely sure what happened in this case, and that is why I asked you to come and discuss the matter with me. We want to be as helpful and unobtrusive as we can."

"I certainly hope so," Borgman said, obviously liking

this less and less. "I must say that I think you are making far too much about this incident."

Gideon raised his head, and thrust his chin forward. Bell glanced swiftly at Lee, recognising the sign of Gideon suddenly switching to the attack. His voice became deeper, his right hand clenched on the desk.

"This incident, Mr Borgman? *In*cident? You call the death of two people an '*in*cident'? I am afraid I take a very different view of the sanctity of human life. If anyone else was even partly responsible for the death of Samuel and his wife, then I want to know who, and I want to see him punished. That is why I am here—to make sure that criminals are punished. I don't like to hear you dismiss death so lightly. There is even the possibility—"

He broke off, creating a kind of menace in the way he left the word hovering. He came nearer to exulting than he ever allowed himself. His years of thinking about Borgman seemed to come to boiling point, and he was intent on scoring every point he could, piling innuendo upon innuendo.

Perhaps the death of Samuel had gone deeper in Borgman than he knew; possibly his visit here had carried his mind back to his first wife's death, and touched him with foreboding. Conceivably he had sent that nurse and her fiancé away, and used the Samuel 'incident' deliberately so as to try to find out whether he had any cause for fear.

He knew, now.

He was sitting very still, as if fighting to keep his composure; he would lose his temper very easily when opposed, perhaps when he was frightened. He could not hide the fact that his hands were tightly clenched. The bright daylight on his face showed that he had paled; and his mouth was compressed and his eyes were narrowed all the time. He glanced at Bell, who was staring at him openly; Bell looked away and began to write.

"What other possibility is there?" Borgman demanded.

Gideon seemed to relax, and his voice lost the stern, accusing tone.

"Perhaps I shouldn't have said that, Mr Borgman, but

there is no reason why you should not know the official view, provided you keep it entirely confidential. In a case of violent death there is always the possibility that it is a matter of foul play. Of murder." He made an infinitesimal pause, just long enough to give the word emphasis; and if this man were a murderer, the way the words came out must feel like hammer blows. "Samuel may have poisoned himself and his wife. That is what the circumstances indicate. But even when it appears to be, poison is not always self-administered, Mr Borgman. They may not have known what they were drinking. There was time for anyone else involved to have found out their danger, and to have gone to the Samuels' house and prepared the poison. I don't say that happened: simply that the possibility must be investigated. If there is one thing which must not go unpunished, it is murder."

He seemed so heavy-handed and ponderous, but the feeling of excitement increased, even grew into one of triumph. The right word, the right implication, seemed to come naturally to his tongue. It was not really hot in there, but now there was a film of perspiration at Borgman's forehead and the short upper lip. Bell had noticed it; Bell also looked buoyant with suppressed excitement.

Borgman spoke deep in his throat.

"I don't believe that there is any question of foul play. I think you are making a great fuss over nothing."

"Nothing?" Gideon echoed, as if shocked. "Nothing?" He paused again, briefly, and then became brisk. "Mr Borgman, if you are right I shall be the first to apologise, but from what Mr Appleby tells me, there is a distinct possibility that these frauds go deeper than you had realised. We must make sure. We can send a squad over to your offices for them to make a thorough and very quick investigation, taking no more than two or three days but causing a great deal of inconvenience, or we can arrange for Superintendent Lee and an assistant to come in as if they were accountants, checking thoroughly but taking longer to do so. Which do you prefer, sir?"

Until then, Gideon felt a deep satisfaction with the

success of his tactics, by the indication that Borgman had been forced into a corner, taken so much by surprise that he had not attempted to fight his way out; at best, he was keeping fear and uncertainty out of his expression. If *only* he dared to make a charge now, Gideon believed he might be able to force some kind of an admission, or hint of admission, out of Borgman.

Almost on the instant that he thought so, Borgman's manner changed. He had absorbed the full weight of the attack, and no longer wilted. In fact he seemed to gain in stature. The metamorphosis showed in his manner, in the tautening of his expression and the glint in his eyes. Now Gideon saw those qualities which Appleby had sensed in the man; a kind of capacity for corruption.

"I think all of this is completely unnecessary," Borgman said bitingly. "I did not expect pompous nonsense from Scotland Yard. Is the Assistant Commissioner for Crime in his office?"

Immediately, Gideon closed up.

"I can find out, sir."

"Do so, at once," Borgman said. "I won't waste more time here."

That was the moment when the battle was really joined; when Gideon decided to 'forget' that the exhumation order had been cancelled.

He said: "Go and see if Mr Rogerson is in, Superintendent, will you?" He waited for Fred Lee to go out, and noticed that Bell was writing more slowly; in fact, he was only pretending to write. Both he and Lee would have been quick to sense the change in Borgman, and to know the weight of the opposition; but that breach had nearly been made.

Borgman went to the window and stood looking over the plane trees, some leaves already turning colour. Obviously he had determined not to talk to Gideon any more, as obviously he was hoping to establish his superiority. There was a supercilious expression in his eyes and at his lips when he turned round as the door opened and Rogerson came in; and he spoke before the door closed.

"Are you the Assistant Commissioner for Crime?"

"Yes." Rogerson could be cold and cutting, but he was a little grey, a little plump, a little fading.

"This officer . . ." began Borgman, and briefly summarised what Gideon had said about the need to investigate at the office, briskly and with complete accuracy. "I regard it as quite unnecessary," he went on. "The facts speak for themselves. A weak-willed and untrustworthy man robbed my company for years and, when faced with it, hadn't the courage to accept punishment. I see no need to take further action beyond the formalities necessary at the inquests. This man committed the crimes, remember—of embezzlement and murder."

He was used to getting his own way, to his word being law; and was prepared to try to make it law here.

"A thorough investigation is absolutely necessary, Mr Borgman," Rogerson said, still coldly.

"I've told Mr Borgman that we can carry out the investigation with great discretion," Gideon put in.

If Borgman fought any more, he would be a fool.

He said curtly: "You may use which method you like. The sooner this farce is over, the sooner your men can concentrate on more necessary work."

"Thank you, Mr Borgman," Gideon said smoothly. "We are anxious not to make too much fuss, and I'll send Superintendent Lee and his assistant along. You will make sure that all the books are open to his inspection, won't you?"

"I will make the necessary arrangements," Borgman promised, obviously finding it hard to be civil, and the atmosphere was frigid when he left, accompanied by Lee.

"What do you make of that, George?" Rogerson asked heavily, when the door was closed.

"Want me to guess?" asked Gideon very slowly.

"Yes."

"All right," said Gideon. "He's been so used to riding roughshod over all opposition that he thinks he's a law to himself. Add his money and his friends, and he's next door to a megalomaniac. What Borgman wants, he'll take. I scared him for ten minutes, but that's all."

"Still think you could make a charge stick without cast-iron evidence?" Rogerson demanded.

"Sooner or later, we'll get him," Gideon said, "and the chances are we'll hate ourselves for not getting him earlier." There was a moment of tense silence, before Rogerson changed the subject abruptly.

"Any news of that killer driver of Soho?"

"No."

"The thing that gets under my skin is that he can't be far away," Rogerson said, obviously ill-at-ease. "Anything else in of importance? I ought to get off soon."

"Nothing that can't keep," Gideon said.

Half an hour later, he drove out of the Yard on to the Embankment. There was little traffic, it was a pleasantly warm evening, and the only car that caught his attention was a black Morris, the same model as the killer car. He felt almost bitter towards Rogerson, who wasn't with him over Borgman; it was the first time he had really clashed with his chief. He was glad in a way that he had one other deep preoccupation. Every time he passed a garage, or even a petrol pump, he found himself wondering if the driver of the killer car had ever filled up there. The truism might be dull but it was inescapable: among the people whom Gideon passed on his drive home there were many criminals; some known, more unknown, and among them there might be the men responsible for the organised car thefts.

* * * * *

In actual fact, the driver of the car that had killed a man that day was in a garage which Gideon passed, not far from the district of south-west London known as World's End.

His name was Larkin.

There was a cut on his forehead, covered with a patch, and another cut on the back of his right hand, although this was not so deep or sharp, because he had been wearing cotton gloves. These gloves, blood-stained, were screwed up in a ball in the wastepaper basket in the little glass-partitioned office of the garage.

Another man, very short and very broad, was sitting behind a littered desk. Two ash-trays and the lid of a paint tin were filled with ash and cigarette ends, which were sometimes emptied into the wastepaper basket, and sometimes left until they were full to over-flowing. The office was not only dusty but dirty, and even the old-fashioned typewriter was thick with dust, except on the keys and the roller.

"You can talk till you're blue in the face," Larkin was saying, "I'm not going to do another job until the heat's off. That cop saw me, don't you get it? I ought to go away for a couple of weeks, and if anyone's earned a holiday, I have."

"Not with pay, Larky," retorted the broad-shouldered man. "You only get paid if you work. I've fixed the alibi for this afternoon's job, so you can forget it. When you've got your nerve back, come and see me."

"Listen, Chas, I'm flat broke! I was relying on the pony for today's job—"

"You didn't do the job, you made a muck of it," said the broad-shouldered man. He took out a battered wallet, counted out ten one-pound notes, and pushed them across the desk. "You can think yourself lucky to have ten. Every time you bring a car in you can count on fifty. So long." He pushed his chair back and picked up a telephone, which was grey with dust except where he handled it. He dialled a number with great deliberation while Larkin watched; and after listening for a moment, he said into the mouthpiece: "Benjie? . . . I've got a vacancy for a driver, got anyone lined up yet? . . . How old? Sure, I'll give him a trial, try anything once. You know me." He tapped the ash off his cigarette. "What's his name? Reggie Cole, okay. He know the drill? . . . Sure, I'll leave it to you."

The broad-shouldered man rang off, and Larkin went slowly out of the office, nursing his injured hand, forgetting the blood-stained gloves in the wastepaper basket.

CHAPTER 8

BIRTH OF TWO CRIMINALS

"REGGIE," Mrs Cole said.

"Yes, Mum."

"Where are you going tonight?"

"Pictures, I suppose."

"You're always going to the pictures; anyone would think your own home wasn't good enough for you. Why don't you stay in and look at the television tonight for a change?"

"It's not the same," Reggie Cole said smoothly. "Won't be late, Mum. Good-night."

He went out of the four-roomed flat in a big, brown block on a new estate in Chelsea, whistling under his breath and feeling the relief that always came when he was away from his home. It was a good enough home in many ways, but these days he simply did not like it. The truth was that his mother and father and his two younger sisters treated him as if he were still a boy, whereas he was eighteen, he had his driving licence, and actually drove a van for his living. His life had changed completely from the moment he had obtained that job; at the wheel of the van or a car, he felt as if he were on top of the world.

And there was Ethel.

Whenever he thought of Ethel, his heart began to beat faster, and he had a choky feeling. He had felt like that almost from the first moment he had seen her, a month ago, when he had called at a garage in Chiswick for some petrol. She had been standing near the garage watching him, a girl who was probably five or six years older than he—that was why he was astonished that she still took such an interest in him—and really something. He often pictured her on that warm day, wearing a sleeveless flowered dress cut low at the front, and with the kind of figure that made his mother shake her head and purse her lips, and at which his father glanced quickly and furtively. Ethel had—well, everything. The way her waist curved in and out was out of this world, and her ankles and legs—phew!

As he had stared at her, unable to make himself look away, she had sauntered over. She had a swaying walk, and he found himself wondering what she would be like from behind. He could recall the vivid red of her lips and the clear skin and beautiful blue eyes, and could almost hear her voice as she had said:

"Going up the West End, by any chance?"

"Why, I–yes, I am. Can I–can I give you a lift?"

"That's exactly what I was hoping," Ethel had said, and when she was sitting next to him, her leg pressing against his, she had told him that she was broke, absolutely flat broke, but she did not like getting lifts from ordinary men: *he* looked so honest.

Ethel . . .

She had seemed so embarrassed when he had offered to lend her a pound or two, but had accepted, and insisted that they should meet the next evening, when she would be able to pay him back. They had met, she had paid him back, they had gone to the Hammersmith Palais, and Reggie had hardly thought it possible that anyone could dance so perfectly, so excitingly; it was as if she *loved* the pressure of his body against her.

That had been six weeks ago.

He knew everything about Ethel now. That she was an actress, waiting for her big chance—but how difficult it was to get work without paying for it in a way no decent girl would consider! She had an invalid mother to look after. She hated accepting money from him, but as soon as she got the big chance she would pay it back ten-fold. When that day came they would not have to drive round in a van, but would have a car of their own—*their* own—and who could tell, it might even be a Jaguar!

Reggie did not recall exactly how much money Ethel had "borrowed" from him, but he did know that he was now heavily in debt; he himself had borrowed from everyone he could tap, and had even tried to borrow from home, although there was never any spare money there. His father was a ten-pounds-a-week house decorator, and that was hardly enough to feed and clothe everybody. So far, Reggie had managed to pay his mother the two pounds a week they had agreed out of his six pounds salary, but he wouldn't be able to pay her this week.

He had just enough silver to buy two coffees and a sandwich as well as pay for the tickets to the *Palais*. That was all Ethel really wanted, and if he couldn't do that for her, what would she think of him?

She was usually at the Tropic Bar waiting for him, and his heart was pounding when he got off the bus near it. Already a stream of youths was going into the dance hall, and outside a loudspeaker was playing the latest dance hit, while huge, lurid-looking posters were splashed about the drab, grey brick of the hall.

There she was!

He waved to her through the window, and she waved back but did not smile. That puzzled and perturbed him. Had he done anything wrong last night? He gulped as he went into the hot, steamy coffee bar. The seat next to Ethel was empty, and he slid on to it and pressed her hand.

"Hallo, Ethel."

"Hallo, Reg."

"Eth, what's the matter?"

"I–I've had a bit of a shock, that's all."

"Nothing I've done, is it?"

"Of course it isn't." She leaned against him, and the scent of her perfume seemed heady, while the yielding touch of her breast sent fire through him. Her hair brushed his cheek for a moment, and he had an idea that she did not want to look at him. "I'm in an awful jam, Reg."

"You mean—money?" He had hardly had time to feel relieved before this new worry was presented.

"Yes," she answered.

"How–how much, Ethel?" He was acutely conscious

of his empty pockets, and there was a kind of despair in him, that he might have to tell her that there was nothing that he could do to help. It might be as much as ten pounds. He found himself wondering desperately how he could lay his hands on that amount, when Ethel blurted out:

"Twenty-five quid."

"*What?*"

"I know, it's awful," Ethel said, and her hands met his and held them tightly. "It's mounted up over the weeks, that's the trouble; I've just had to borrow for my mother's sake, and I went to a moneylender. He lent me fifteen pounds and it's grown to twenty-five before I could look round. If I don't pay up tomorrow, he'll come to the flat. I don't know what would happen if he did; my mother simply couldn't stand the shock."

Reggie muttered: "It's a hell of a lot of money; I just don't see how I can lay my hands on it. I'd give anything in the world if I could—I'd do anything."

Ethel looked at him with her brilliant eyes, her red lips parted a little, as if breathlessly, and the white of her teeth just showing; she was truly a beauty in a buxom way, and tonight she wore a dress which was high at the neck, but had no sleeves; she had beautifully rounded white arms.

"Would you, Reggie?"

"You know I would."

She moistened her lips. "I–I asked a friend of mine if he would help, and he said he knew a way of getting his hands on fifty if I could drive a car. But I can't drive."

Reggie's eyes lit up. "Well, that's easy, then! I can drive a car; it's simple. There isn't a car in the world I can't drive," Reggie boasted, and in that moment he believed it. "Just show me what to do, and I'll do it."

"Why don't you keep your voice down?" a man asked from just behind him. Reggie swung round on his stool, and saw a little dark-haired, sallow man with a turnip-shaped forehead, standing close by. "Take it easy, now; I'm Ethel's pal, and I can make easy money for you, if you'll do what I tell you," this sallow intruder said. "There's no risk in it, not really; you just have to be able to drive and keep your wits about you. How about it?"

Reggie asked: "What–what *is* this job?"

The man had very small pupils which looked almost black, and the whites of his eyes were huge and yellowish. He gave a little sneering smile, but didn't speak. There was no need to speak, really. No one paid fifty pounds for a 'job' unless it was risky, and that meant breaking the law. But there was Ethel, sitting so helpless and hopeless, her hand on his; and she was leaning against him.

There wasn't anything he wouldn't do for Ethel.

"You just get into a car and drive it to a certain place, where it will be taken over," the little man said. "I know the car, and I know where it is. When you've delivered it, there'll be fifty quid on the nail. Cash. How about it?"

Ethel pressed harder against Reggie's shoulder. His mouth was very dry, and his heart was beating fast again, while his lips were sticky. For the first time he had a feeling that Ethel had been egging him on to this, and that once he was in, it wouldn't be easy to get out. This was a moment of decision, and he could go whichever way he chose.

He moistened his lips.

"Show me the car, and I'll drive it," he said.

* * * * *

Half an hour later, he walked towards an Austin A70 which was parked near the corner of a street in Chelsea. There were dozens of cars near by, for this was quite near two cinemas and a theatre. He had two ignition keys in his pocket, and was assured that one or the other would switch on the engine, and that he would find that the door was open. As he walked towards the car, he felt as if a thousand pairs of eyes were turned towards him. A man and a woman came walking along slowly, arm in arm, and he thought that they were staring at him. Two men came, briskly. There was a public-house on a corner opposite, and a man and woman came hurrying out of that towards the cars; *towards this car?* He was beetroot red when he walked past it. The couple got into a car some distance along, and Reggie turned back.

No one was in sight now.

He was acutely aware of the windows of the houses on either side of the street, and of the possibility that a door would open and someone would come to the car. But now was the time. When he strode to the car he was shivering and yet his head felt hot. He depressed the handle and pulled, and the door opened. He darted a glance up and down, and then slid into the seat and slammed the door. For a moment he was trembling so much that he did not think he would be able to keep the keys steady, but he made himself. The metal of the key scratched on the ignition, and it seemed an age until he had pushed it in. A girl hurried past, swinging a tennis racket. He pushed the key right in and turned, but it did not work. He began to mutter to himself and was clenching his teeth so hard that his jaws ached. He tried the second key—and it turned and the ignition glowed.

Now, his heart began to pound.

He pressed the self-starter, and it worked at once. He glanced into the driving mirror, knowing there was good room to manœuvre. Quite suddenly, he felt cool, aware of no panic and no trembling. The wheel of a car had always affected him like that. He put the gear into reverse as if he had been driving this particular car for weeks, went back a little, and got out of the parking position at the first turn. As he began to press the accelerator and gain speed, he felt a surge of excitement. At twenty miles an hour, he swung into the road; nothing was coming in either direction. He drove a little faster, and then turned towards Sloane Square and the street where he had been told to leave the car, with the ignition key in it.

"Why, it was easy," he told himself chokily. "It was dead easy? If that's worth fifty quid—"

He didn't finish.

When he reached the appointed place, he got out of the car and walked towards the furthest corner, as he had been told. A little man in a raincoat, the man who had been at the coffee bar, was leaning against the wall. Reggie knew exactly what to do, and did it: he walked straight past, taking a small bundle from the other's hands as he did so. It was not until he was in a shop doorway in King's Road that he opened the envelope and looked inside.

There was the money; fifty soiled one-pound notes—about fifty, anyhow.

He could not get to Ethel quickly enough. He had got her out of trouble, and there was no telling how she would say thanks. He was a man, wasn't he? He was eighteen. Fellows actually got married at eighteen.

* * * * *

Nearer the heart of London, in Victoria, a young man of twenty-three was standing at the bar of a small, select club, with a glass in front of him, and a blonde by his side. His name was Arthur Kingsley, and he had never heard of Reggie Cole, who was from a different world. Kingsley had been to one of the lesser known public schools. He knew that his parents had sacrificed much to pay the fees, and it had never occurred to him that he was ungrateful. They lived in the country, in a little cottage, and he was on a newspaper as a sporting correspondent at a fantastically low salary—less than fifteen pounds a week. There was the rent of his flat to pay, five pounds a week, and the odds and ends that had to be met, and by the time he had finished the normal weekly payments on his television, a daily help, his food and laundry, he had only two or three pounds left. He didn't drink much at home because he couldn't afford it, but he had to spend more freely at the club. Either he had to mix with his own set, or else cut loose; and he could not bring himself to do that.

It was not because of any particular girl; girls were two-a-penny, in bed or out. It was the *métier*: this kind of club, with its fat entrance fee and its high prices, mixing with men who were really well off, who talked in thousands when he thought in tens; meeting the kind of people he had known for years. This was his world, and he belonged here; yet he was practically broke. He had borrowed on his insurance, borrowed from the few friends who had money, sold a typewriter and a watch—and now he was really up against it. He could not even stand a round of drinks cheerfully, because a big round would tip him further into the red, and he had chalked up to his limit.

If he didn't stand his round, on the other hand, he would be a laughing stock. He had seen it happen to others who had tried to make the grade but could not. The best thing was to find some excuse for leaving early.

He was trying to make up his mind to go when Soames came out of the office. The manager was a tall, lean man, fair-haired, with a fresh look about him, more the outdoor than the indoor type; he had a good reputation as a tennis player and was known to be a gambler, mostly on horses. He treated everyone exactly alike: millionaire and Arthur Kingsley, duke and chorus girl. Kingsley thought uneasily that Soames was probably coming this way, and might even be coming to speak to him. Surely he wasn't going to mention that bill? Usually anyone with too much on the slate was called to the office, and he hadn't been called. It was all done so smoothly and pleasantly, but it was a fact that very few members who went to the office showed up next day.

Soames came straight to Kingsley, who was the more heavily-built man, a rugged type to look at. He had played for the public schools at both Rugby and cricket. Now Kingsley felt as if the room were stiflingly hot, and he could not think clearly. He probably owed nearer fifty than forty pounds, but it couldn't be seriously more than fifty. A girl with brassy-coloured hair, who bulged in a strapless cocktail dress, caught Soames' arm and cooed: "Peter, darling, it's so long since I've seen you." Soames talked to her for a few minutes, small talk which meant nothing, while she pouted up at him. Then he disengaged himself courteously, and came up to Kingsley.

"Hallo, Mr Kingsley," he greeted, and his even smile was friendly enough. "Are you likely to be going to Epsom tomorrow?"

Kingsley was so astounded that he almost shouted: "Well, yes, as a matter of fact I am."

"I wonder if you'll carry out a little commission for me," Soames said. "I want to back Black Eye at starting price if it's better than tens, and I think it will be. I can't get away to handle it myself."

Kingsley was still on the verge of shouting.

"Well, yes, I'll be glad to! Can't say my money will be on Black Eye, but if you think it's a good thing I might change my mind."

"Come into my office and have a look at the form," suggested Soames, and led the way. Kingsley felt dazed and bewildered as he followed, more bewildered when Soames poured out a whisky and soda and raised his glass. "Cheers." They drank. "Kingsley, I hope you won't mind my being frank," Soames went on, and immediately Kingsley's alarm returned, and he went tense, "but you're a bit short of cash, aren't you?"

"Well, yes, but it won't last," Kingsley made himself say. "I'm in line for promotion any time now, and that will be worth at least another five hundred a year. That would put me in funds. I assure you that I won't leave my account standing too long."

"I could put you in the way of an extra hundred a month, no questions asked, no tax, no worries," Soames said easily.

"It sounds too good to be true!" Kingsley felt a flare of excitement which echoed in his voice.

"It's true all right," Soames assured him. "It's simply a matter of taking a slight risk. It mustn't be done too often—just a killing now and again, and my principals will find it well worth that hundred a month. It's simply a question of slipping a little stuff into the right place—anyone who's trusted can do it, and you've got a first-class reputation."

"You mean—*doping* a horse?"

"Just pepping it up a bit, or unpepping it," Soames said, and gave his most pleasant smile. He had the look of the glamorised young Nazi: the same upright back, the same flat head, the same spare body and square shoulders, and he always seemed to be at attention. "Everything will be arranged, and you'll be told what horse to fix in good time. You'll be given the dope in liquid form and all you have to do is get it into the water the horse drinks. There's not a chance in a thousand of being caught, provided it isn't done too often."

Kingsley moistened his lips.

"How–how often?"

"Oh–two or three times a year," said Soames. He went to his beautifully-figured walnut desk, took out a loose-leaf book, turned the pages deliberately, and then came to one which Kingsley saw was headed with his name. "I see you've chalked up sixty-four pounds ten," Soames went on. "To show that I'm serious, I'll mark this paid, and advance you the first month's allowance. You have only to say the word."

He opened a drawer and took out a bundle of new one-pound notes, fresh and crisp, and held together with a brown paper band. He ran his thumb over the edge of these and they made a whirring sound, like a pack of cards being bent back and then allowed to flip forward. He put the bundle on the desk, smiled up, and said:

"How does it sound?"

"Supposing–supposing I don't manage to do it?" Kingsley said huskily.

"You'll find a way," Soames declared confidently. "You'll find the principals very understanding and helpful, too. It's simply a matter of co-operation. If there's a big win, you'll get a cut in it. Shall I cross off this account?"

Kingsley said: "Yes. Yes, please. I'll do the best I can."

* * * * *

The smell of the horses, the air of excitement, the sight of the jockeys and the trainers, the smell of leather, all of these things were like a drug to Kingsley, and that morning he felt a fierce excitement to go with it; and nervousness, too. He had been told how best to put the tiny soluble capsule of liquid into a pail of water; had practised on his own, and was quite sure that he could get away with it. No one seemed in the slightest degree suspicious, but when he actually let the capsule fall in he felt a moment of panic, and had to force himself to stand still. There were three people within sight, but none of them took the slightest notice of him, and the capsule disappeared beneath the surface at once. He moved away. An hour later, he stood in the enclosure, glasses at his eyes, watching the bunch of horses tearing round Tattenham Corner to the straight. The excitement of the crowd, the roaring, the sun shining on the motley, were all almost non-existent: he had doped a 25 to 1 outsider, and had been told that with the dope it could not fail to win. It was Disc, with a young apprentice up, and no one really gave it a chance. He saw the colours, green, red and white hoops, in the middle of the bunch; five horses were all very close together. Then he saw Disc begin to surge forward, saw the apprentice make for a gap in the rails, heard the sudden hush as the crowd watched the favourite being overhauled. Teeth gritting, hands clenched, fingers like steel bands round the glasses, Kingsley saw Disc sweep past and pass the post two lengths ahead of the field.

And he had put twenty-five pounds on it; twenty-five pounds at 25 to 1. He had made a fortune!

* * * * *

Mixing with the thousands on the heath were Surrey C.I.D. men as well as some special squads from Scotland Yard, all on the look-out for pickpockets and con-men. The sun was warm, men carried their coats and jackets, women in light cotton dresses had their handbags hanging over their arms. Grey topper was next to cloth cap, the latest Dior next to a dress from Marks and Spencer. Sunshine reflected from the thousands of cars, making a sprawling rainbow of colour—and sunshine reflected from the glasses of a man who was making his way towards the motor-cycle park on the Downs. He was looking towards the ground all the time, and in spite of the heat he wore a raincoat and a trilby hat pulled rather low over his eyes. Now and again he glanced up and round, as if afraid that he was being followed, but no one appeared to take any particular notice of him.

At that moment, no one was.

His name was Carslake, and two weeks ago he had murdered a man named Robson, because he was in love with Robson's wife. Until yesterday he had thought there was a chance of getting away with it, but the morning's papers had been full of the discovery of the body, and his own photograph had been in several of them, with the ominous words: '*Hector Carslake, whom the police think may be able to help in inquiries.*' He did not know what to do. He had only a little money, and doubted whether he could get out of the country, for he had never had a passport. His chief hope was that he could get to Ireland; he had a feeling that a stretch of water would help to make him safe.

He had come here partly because he spent most of his free time at the races or studying form, and he had lost two pounds on the first four races, when hoping desperately to make enough to last him for several weeks.

He was a biggish man, slightly splay-footed.

He pushed between the rows of motor-cycles and motor-scooters, looking for an old one which would not be conspicuous, and which he could wheel away easily and so get a good start. He believed that there were so many people on the Downs that he would get away; there was safety in numbers, he kept telling himself; it was easy to get lost in a crowd.

He spotted an old Norton, with the paint badly scratched and the rubber of the pedals worn smooth. He stopped by it. No one was near. He held the handlebars and released the stand, then wheeled the heavy machine into the path where he could ride it. He stared down at the ground all the time, not daring to look up in case a car-park attendant or one of the policemen saw him, and came to make sure that it was his machine. Now that he was on the point of riding away, he was near panic.

Some way off, a detective sergeant from one of the South London Divisions glanced towards the motor-cycle park, when the sun glinted on a man's glasses, a hundred yards or so away. The sergeant, named Miles, was feeling very hot in his brown serge suit, although he wore no waistcoat, and part of the time he carried his hat because his head became sticky with sweat. Yet over there was a man wearing a trilby pulled low over his forehead, the only man in sight wearing a raincoat, and who stared fixedly at the ground.

Miles, wise in police work, strolled casually towards the spot where the motor-cyclist would come on his way out. He made no sign that he was interested, and took off his hat and wiped his forehead of sweat. He actually turned his back on the motor-cycle as it started up, but swung round when it was close to him.

The driver was staring at him.

"That's Carslake!" Miles exclaimed aloud, and was so astonished that he lost a moment, and so threw away the advantage of full surprise. For a moment the man on the machine and the man on foot stared at each other.

Miles moved forward. "Just a minute!"

Carslake opened the throttle with a jerky movement, and the motor-cycle leapt forward. There was hardly room for it to pass between Miles and the hedge. The engine roared. Miles knew that if he flung himself at the man and machine he might be seriously injured; Carslake knew that if he were caught here he would not have a chance. He wanted to strike out, he wanted to *kill*, he wanted to run this man down. He turned the wheel of the motor-cycle towards the man—at the precise moment that Miles pulled a whistle from his pocket, blew on it, and then jumped forward. He made a sweeping blow with his right arm, trying to fend off the motor-cycle with his left. There was a split second when Miles, Carslake and the machine seemed to merge into a strange, futuristic, writhing shape; and then the motor-cycle toppled over. Carslake went with it, tried to get clear but felt the weight of it crush his left leg; he screamed with pain and felt something snap. Miles moved back, left hand cut on the mudguard of the machine, but otherwise unhurt. Men were running, two of them in police uniform, and he knew that there was no risk at all that Carslake would escape.

Then he realised that the man was badly injured, and he went forward to help him.

* * * * *

At half past four that afternoon, Gideon's telephone bell rang, and he stopped pushing the lawnmower over the little patch of grass at the front of his house, drew his white shirt sleeve across his forehead, and went indoors. Kate was out shopping in Fulham Market; all the family were out, too. The bell kept ringing, and for once he almost resented it. He had lost himself in the gardening, but this interruption brought Borgman and the clash with Rogerson back vividly.

"All right, all right," he said testily, and snatched up the receiver. "Gideon."

"Hallo, George," said a man in a cheerful Cockney voice. "Didn't spoil your forty winks, I hope. Gotta bitta good for you."

"Time you had, Lem," Gideon said, and immediately felt better. "What is it? Borgman confessed?"

"That'll be the day. No, we've got Carslake. He's admitted that he killed Robson, and says that the woman knew nothing about it. We could pull her in, or we could leave her. What do you think we ought to do?"

"Leave it to Hoppy," Gideon said promptly. "No point in throwing our weight about with him. Anything else in?"

"I went down two quid on a dead cert at Epsom," the other man, Lemaitre, said. He had once been Gideon's chief *aide*, but recently had been moved from night duty to a kind of roving commission, and was in charge at the Yard during weekends. "A 25 to 1 outsider romped home. Some people have all the luck. Tell you why I really called, though."

"Why?"

"There's that stolen car report. Info's finished it and it's on your desk. Like to have it at home for the weekend?"

"Yes. Anything in about the killer motorist?"

"I've been studying the reports from the people who've been questioned," Lemaitre said. "Seven think they saw him, and he looked different to each one. We're going to be lucky! Tell you what, though. I've seen the lab report on the cotton from that splinter of glass. Egyptian cotton, almost certainly made in Japan, and they're selling for three-and-elevenpence in every cheap store in the country. Blood group A. The lab's got a couple of pairs, and they're trying to find out if the strand came out of a finger, a thumb, or the main part of the glove."

"Good," said Gideon. "That the lot?"

"No."

"Remember this is my afternoon off," Gideon said, and hooked a chair near with his foot and sat down.

"That's why I hesitated to call you, Commander," said Lemaitre, in a tone of highly concentrated sarcasm. "But there was one little thing I thought you'd like to know about, apart from all the jobs you left over for me to do while you were snoozing. The autopsy report's in from the Berkshire boys on the Borgman corpus."

Gideon caught his breath, and it was nearly half a minute before he said:

"What is it?"

"Enough morphine to have killed a dozen people," Lemaitre answered. "Good thing the autopsy wasn't called off."

CHAPTER 9

GROUNDS FOR A CHARGE

"It was a bloody silly thing to do, George," Rogerson said, "and it's no use telling me that you forgot; elephants don't. But after this I suppose you'll get your own way." He pushed the pathologist's report aside, and gave Gideon a quick grin. "One in the eye for the Home Office, too. Think anyone's got the story about the exhumation?"

"It's not in any of the papers," Gideon said. "It was a sleepy little village, remember, and they did it at night. No one picked the thing up for the Press so far. Borgman's still in Paris."

"Alone?"

Gideon said: "His secretary, the girl named Clare Selby, isn't at home this weekend. Mrs Borgman is."

"You may be more right than you know," conceded Rogerson, and looked very thoughtful. "George, you made me feel a heel over the exhumation."

"Forget it."

"Well, what do you think we ought to do?"

Gideon said: "I've sent Freddy Lee and Carmichael to Borgman's offices, and they'll be started by now. Borgman isn't due back until tomorrow, although his secretary is on her way back now—he takes the trouble to try not to make the *affaire* too obvious. What I would do is to let the news of the exhumation leak into the papers tomorrow, so that it will greet Borgman when he gets back—wouldn't be a bad idea to try to get some newspapermen to meet him off the plane, and ask him if he's got any comment to make. When he gets to his office, our chaps will be there. He'll be looking over his shoulder all the time, and wondering what they're really doing—wondering whether we were ever really interested in what Samuel did, or whether we're just after him. Meanwhile, Fred Lee can dig all day about this Clare Selby girl, and anything else on Borgman. I've had a good look at the first reports on Borgman's present wife," Gideon went on. "He used to take her everywhere, but these days he usually travels by himself. She's worth nearly a hundred thousand pounds, too."

"Borgman must be worth a million."

"That doesn't mean that he's got a million of ready money," Gideon said, dryly. "Anyway, I'll get everything checked—and then I think we ought to leave Borgman for a couple of days, perhaps the better part of a week, but have him followed wherever he goes."

"We'll try it, anyhow," Rogerson said. "I'll put the case up to the Old Man, and leave it to him. But after this report I don't see how anyone could advise us not to charge him, even if we don't find Nurse Kennett. George, you look five years younger."

Gideon smiled soberly.

"I want Borgman," he said simply. "When that man's off my shoulder, I'll feel better." In his mind's eye he seemed to see an image of the nurse who had disappeared. "Got time for the rest of the weekend stuff?"

"I've twenty minutes."

"It'll do. First there's Carslake . . ." Gideon talked with his usual deliberation, making full use of every word, drawing a graphic picture of the weekend's crime, including developments in the cases which had been held over the previous week. After ten minutes, he said: "There are only two left that matter. Red and Syd Carter are coming up for the second hearing on Friday. I think there's plenty of evidence, and we ought to apply for committal for trial. No point in wasting time, and we could do with a headline or two."

"Go ahead," Rogerson agreed.

"Ta. Then there's the car thefts," Gideon went on, and began to drum his fingers on Rogerson's large desk. "There were five from Epsom on Saturday, and seventeen in all from football crowds, seven from greyhound tracks at night, and four from cinemas."

"This isn't a crime, this is an industry."

"That's what's worrying me," Gideon said. "If anything ever gets under my skin, it's when we come across a job which has been going on for months, maybe for years, under our noses. I spent most of Sunday studying the figures—and there are nearly five hundred cars on the stolen list, covering the four-week period. Only two hundred have been recovered, and they were nearly all stripped of accessories, tyres, the usual. That leaves three hundred unaccounted for. Most mid-week thefts come from the West End, most weekend jobs from the suburbs. Let's say that thirty or forty were just the usual fly-by-night jobs, and we've got the three hundred stolen cars vanishing without a trace in a month. They're being painted all right, so there's your industry. There must be a dozen garages, perhaps more, working on the job."

Rogerson looked as if he were trying to absorb the full significance of all this.

"And some of those garages must be run by the same group," Gideon argued. "I can see three or four unconnected garages handling stolen cars, but a dozen or more—there's a tie-up all right. A lot of them are probably under the same management."

"A chain of garages," Rogerson said heavily.

"That's right," agreed Gideon. "So I'm having Todd check on all groups with six garages or more—better not start too high, and two small chains might be working together—and he should have a report in a couple of days. There's one other thing I'd like to do, though, if we can spare the men."

"Don't know that I like the sound of that," Rogerson said. "What is it?"

Gideon took a small plastic envelope from his pocket and laid it down in front of the Assistant Commissioner. Inside were several strands of grey cotton, and on all the strands little dark brown stains. A label stapled to the envelope read: '*Cotton strands presumably from glove found on glass splinter in Saige Street, Soho—18.9.19—*'

"The killer car job?"

"Yes. The lab's examined half a dozen pairs of gloves

made of the same material—I told you they were Japanese—and they say these strands came from the thumb," said Gideon. "They've got some photo enlargements, showing the curvature of the fabric, how it's stretched, and—"

"I'll take your word for it."

"Thanks. If the driver who wore these went to a garage, one of the first things he would do is to take off the glove and have the cut seen to," Gideon said. "If it were badly blood-stained, he might throw the glove away. The lab says that these strands are soaked in one spot and there must have been considerable bleeding."

"So you want to have all garages visited."

Gideon nodded.

"Why ask me?" inquired Rogerson. "You don't often show such consideration, George."

"Got to get back into your good books somehow!"

"Right." Rogerson also stood up and walked with him to the door. "Not a bad week, all-in-all. The Carters committed for trial, Borgman right under the microscope, Carslake in the bag, Baldy Lock, too—keep it up!"

Gideon said: "Make sure the Old Man doesn't let the politicians talk him out of Borgman, won't you?"

"They can't, now," Rogerson said confidently. "But there is one thing, George—I'm not sure you're wise to have him watched wherever he goes."

Gideon stood solid and massive by the door, fingers on the handle, too experienced a man to reject that comment out of hand, and ready to hear why Rogerson had made it. He himself felt reasonably satisfied with the way things were going, but there was that strangely personal feeling about Borgman, the desire to get the man at all costs; and he knew that it was possible that it disturbed his judgment.

"Not often you don't jump to it," Rogerson said, and spread his hands. "I may be wrong, but if you're having the offices covered, if you let news of the exhumation get out, if you have him questioned at the airport when he gets back tomorrow, then aren't you taking a risk that he'll try to get out of the country? We've a good case for home consumption, but I wouldn't like to say we could get extradition on it."

Gideon said heavily: "I didn't even think of that."

"You would have."

"Too late, probably," Gideon said. "I'll take the men off him anyhow, and I won't push Fleet Street. But because we don't want them to do a thing, they'll probably do it. I hope that girl won't warn him."

"The blonde?"

"Yes," said Gideon, and shrugged his shoulders. "I can't really see Borgman staying out of the country until it all blows over, though. If he stayed away he would be making a kind of confession. He'll be back tomorrow."

'Unless,' thought Gideon, uneasily, as he walked along the wide, bare passage to his own office, 'I've scared him too much already.' There was just a possibility. He pictured Borgman sitting in his, Gideon's, office, the film of sweat at his forehead and his upper lip. He reminded himself that Borgman was both clever and thorough, and that he had agencies and branches in many parts of the world; and funds, too. And there had been that striking change in his manner. If the obsession had made him spring the trap too soon, Gideon thought gloomily, he had only himself to blame. The Home Office was probably already sore about the exhumation, and would want cast-iron proof of Borgman's guilt before they tried to get him from abroad. Only Nurse Kennett seemed to offer that. Where the hell was she? Inquiries about her had been made in all Commonwealth countries, and many others, and there was still no news at all.

Was Rogerson simply being bloody-minded? Was there really any likelihood that Borgman would stay out of the country? Wasn't Rogerson's reasoning a kind of justification for his earlier attitude?

Bell was in the office, on the telephone. He rang off as Gideon sat down, glanced up, and said:

"Rogerson still a bit sore?"

"No," said Gideon. "No. That blonde of Borgman's back yet?"

"Arrived at London airport half an hour ago."

"Something," said Gideon. He sat back in his chair, knowing that Bell was puzzled, and then lifted the internal telephone and said: "Ask Mr Appleby to come in." He waited, and Bell's telephone went again: this was one of the mornings when everything was non-stop. Bell took a message, made notes, and rang off, and the door opened and Appleby arrived.

"Jim, your French is better than anyone's here," said Gideon. "Call one of your Paris pals, will you—LeClerc if you can get him—and ask him to have a quick check on Borgman. Borgman's at the Vido Hotel. Find out if he's been to his bank, or if there's any indication that he might have been planning a long flight."

"Gawd!" Appleby breathed. "Okay, I'll fix it."

Word came in, twenty minutes later, that Borgman's movements were quite unsuspicious. All the weekend a blonde young woman had occupied a room on the same floor as Borgman's at the Vido, which was near the Champs Elysées, and Borgman had had several meals in his room; obviously he was being as discreet as ever. Gideon felt easier in his mind, laid on the calls on all garages in the search for the Japanese cotton glove, checked through more reports, and sent for sandwiches from the canteen. Bell went out to lunch, and Gideon was there alone when the door opened and Fred Lee came in.

"Hallo," Gideon greeted. "Didn't expect you yet. Any trouble?"

"Wouldn't say it's trouble," Lee said, and obviously he was feeling quite pleased with himself. "I haven't been able to dig very deep yet, but Samuel was small time. I doubt if the total defalcations are more than three thousand pounds over the whole period he was at the job. Everything else is in apple-pie order—I should be surprised if you could find anything that would help to fix Borgman from the accounts. They've a good chief accountant, even if he was fooled by Samuel."

"And you don't think that's trouble," Gideon remarked.

"Not really, George." Lee sat on a corner of Gideon's desk, hugging his knees, and there was a little colour in his cheeks, a glint in his eye which told Gideon that he was feeling more himself—and if Lee thought that he had discovered something to help put Borgman away, it really would be a tonic. "Borgman has a slap-up office, panelled walls, desk to match, Old Masters—the millionaire's dream. The desk's full of trick drawers, sliding panels, you-know-what."

Gideon went very still.

"Lucky thing I had Carmichael with me," Lee went on serenely. "Good chap, Carmy. As Borgman and the blonde were away, I got him to take that desk apart. In one of the secret compartments were some powdered morphine and a morphine solution, as well as a hypodermic syringe."

Gideon thumped his desk with a great surge of excitement.

"Then we've got him!"

"Can't imagine he'll ever get away with this," Lee agreed smugly. "Got a little problem though, George. Can't let anyone think we'd do such a thing as that without a search warrant, can we?"

"I'll get a warrant for tomorrow morning, and search the desk while Borgman's there," Gideon said. "This is one time when I can't wait."

* * * * *

Reggie Cole was telling himself that he couldn't wait for the next job; anything which earned him fifty pounds as easily as that was something to pray for. After the first few minutes, he had not really been scared; and he had not had one moment's compunction, no feeling of shame or guilt. Any job which won him the kind of reward he wanted from Ethel was worth ten times as great a risk, anyhow. He was happier than he had ever been driving his delivery van, and he called—as usual—at the garage where he had first met Ethel, to get the tank filled up and the oil checked. He always hoped that he might see Ethel there again, and on one occasion he had.

Ethel wasn't there this morning.

There seemed to be trouble of some kind. Two men were inside the littered office, talking to Bennett, the manager, a square-shouldered, stocky man whom he did not greatly like. A youth came up to serve Reggie, and he asked:

"What's on?"

"Cops," the youth said laconically.

Reggie's heart began to thump. "What's it about?"

"They're looking for a glove."

"For a what?"

"A glove," the boy repeated, "and Bennett told them they were wasting their time, but he didn't like it when they said they was going to look. Funny, if you ask me."

"Yeh," Reggie agreed. "Five gallons and check the levels." He went towards the door of the showroom, seeing the two men moving about the small office and Bennett watching them, scowling. He saw them pick up the wicker wastepaper basket and place it on the desk, then begin to remove all the oddments from it. Then he saw one of the men jerk his head up, and say:

"Look."

He was holding something that looked like a rag. Reggie got closer, and saw the man holding it up by one finger: it was a grey glove, obviously very dirty. Then he picked out another. The man handled them with great care, put them into a cellophane bag, and then sealed the bag while the other man said to Bennett:

"Whose gloves are these?"

"How should I know?" Bennett demanded.

"It's your office, isn't it?"

"I get a lot of visitors."

"Don't be funny, Bennett. Whose gloves are they?"

"I tell you I dunno," Bennett insisted. "I tell you I've never seen them before. They aren't my gloves, I never wear them." He spread out his stubby hands, with the flat, bitten nails, ingrained with black oil; revolting. "I'm not here all the time, either; they might have been put there at night, or when I was out on a job."

The detective turned round, and called: "Here, you, boy." The youngster who was holding the nozzle of the petrol hose in the van's filler jumped so much that a little petrol spilled out.

"Careful!" shouted Bennett. He came over to the van and Reggie saw that he was looking at him intently, but could not understand why. "I'll finish that," Bennett said to the boy; "the *gentlemen* want to talk to you." He took the hose while the boy moved towards the two detectives, stared at the ground and said: "Listen, Cole, there's a quick quid for you if you deliver a message for me pronto."

"Where to?"

"Butterby's Garage, Fulham Road. Tell the manager that Larkin is for it, the cops are after him. Got that?"

"Larkin is for it," Reggie echoed.

"Make it slippy," Bennett urged, and the automatic pump stopped and he took the nozzle out. "Never mind paying me, pay yourself; that'll be nearer two quid."

"I'll go right away," Reggie promised. He gave the detectives a last curious glance, nervously excited, and then drove off, clashing his gears a little when he was turning into the High Street. Fulham Road was only a ten-minute drive away, and he knew Butterby's Garage, although he seldom called there. He pulled up as a tall, lanky man came sauntering towards him.

"You the manager?" Reggie asked.

"Supposing I am."

"I've got a message from Mr Bennett," Reggie said, and saw the other's eyes narrow, as if this wasn't good news. "He says that the cops are after Larkin."

"*Larkin?*" the lanky man exclaimed.

"That's what Mr Bennett said."

"Okay, okay," said the manager, and turned towards the big repair shop, with its collection of tools, old tyres, machines, oil and old rags. One man was in the oil well, beneath a tiny Austin; another was whistling as he turned a lathe and made sparks fly from a wheel nut. "Just keep your mouth shut," the manager called to Reggie, "and you won't regret it. It could be worth more to you than the job last night."

Reggie was a mile down the road before he realised that the manager, a complete stranger, knew about the job of the previous night.

The sense of power that the wheel of a car always gave him was much stronger. He passed two cars and cut in each time, then saw a policeman stare at him. He slowed down; it would be crazy to run into trouble because of speeding. From that moment onwards, he was a little uneasy. He wondered who the man Larkin was, and wondered when he would be able to call at Bennett's Garage again to find out what had happened.

* * * * *

The man Larkin was lying back in an easy chair, his injured right hand bandaged and the thumb looking massive, and listening to radio music from a set tuned low. He was alone in a small house which overlooked a big biscuit factory, with two tall chimneys, one billowing dark smoke. The noise of machinery came clearly across the road, merging with the swing from the radio. Larkin was humming to himself, and his eyes were closed.

The music and the clattering noise drowned the sounds inside the little house. Yet there were sounds. Larkin was oblivious of them until there was a noise at the door, and he opened his eyes and stared at the handle. It was turning. He pushed the radio aside and jumped up from the chair as the door opened.

A small man appeared.

"Cor blimey, Charley, want to frighten me to death?" Larkin demanded. "I never heard you come up the stairs."

"You wouldn't hear if someone was to blow a copper's whistle under your sniffer," the newcomer sneered. "Looked out in the street lately?"

"Whatjer mean?"

"Go and see," advised the small man. "Keep to the side, you clot, you don't want them to see you." He watched Larkin turn and go towards the window, keeping well to one side, and he followed. He took his right hand from beneath his coat as he drew nearer Larkin's back, and he said: "See?"

Larkin was trying to squint down into the street.

"No, I can't see anything. Charley, what—"

Some sixth sense seemed to warn him of danger. He turned his head, and saw a spanner smashing down towards him. He thrust up a hand and squealed with pain. The spanner had smacked on the side of his head enough to knock him to one side, but the unflung arm took part of the blow. Staggering, he tried to shout but could not, and there was frothy saliva at the corners of his mouth.

"Don't–don't–don't—" he tried to say.

The small man pushed his hands aside and struck three times again.

* * * * *

Borgman was alone, at about that time.

The day before, at that hour, Clare had been with him, Clare who looked so cool, almost cold, and yet could reach the heights of physical passion, could even exhaust him. Yesterday. It was a strange fact that until she had left for the airport he had not felt the true weight of fear. With her, he had felt a kind of sanctuary, as if she were part of a new, safe world. Soon after she had gone, everything that had been said at Scotland Yard flooded his mind; as if Clare had held the sluice gates of fear together, and her going had opened them. He had known for a long time that he wanted more than a liaison, but it was only now that he began to realise how desperately he needed her.

He was sitting outside the Hotel de Paris, in the warm afternoon sunshine, surrounded by American and English tourists, by Germans and Italians, and here and there a Frenchman. He had a Dubonnet in front of him, and four cigarette stubs were squashed out in his ash-tray. He was lighting a fifth cigarette when the waiter came up, took away the dirty ash-tray and left a clean one. Borgman hardly noticed that. He was staring at two men who were walking along the pavement with slow, ponderous tread, like the tread of the English policeman. He had seen half a dozen men of this stamp and build at Scotland Yard. He watched them while trying to pretend that he had not noticed them. He felt fear pounding away inside him. Were they coming to see him? Could they really know—

He wiped his forehead.

The men passed, without even glancing at him, and he heard one of them speak in a guttural voice which was certainly not English. He wiped his forehead again, sipped his drink, and paid his check. Then he stepped out beneath the shade of the trees, one of the thousands walking towards the Madeleine. He could sit still no longer; he could not think clearly, could only keep telling himself that Gideon was a pompous fool. There could not have been any real knowledge, not even suspicions, in the Yard man's mind when he had talked about murderers being punished, about old crimes catching up with a man.

Borgman knew one thing that he had not known on Friday; his first wife was not really driven from his mind. He had not thought seriously about her, certainly not thought about the mechanics of murdering her, for a long time. Not since Jane Kennett had gone off as if satisfied with her thousand pounds, but swearing that she would always love him.

He had heard from her a year later, saying she was in Australia, married to a doctor, or living with one, it didn't much matter.

She was the only person living who knew that he had murdered Leah.

He had approached the idea of murdering Charlotte as if Leah's murder had been one he had read about, not actually committed. But the visit to Gideon and the Yard had brought his first wife vividly to life.

She had never realised that he had caused the accident; she had been so pathetically glad to see him, had told him exactly what had happened, had rejoiced in his failure to kill her off. He remembered the doctor saying that she might have a sudden relapse, it wouldn't surprise him; he remembered asking Jane Kennett to get the morphia from the dispensary—and how she had. Now he could only think of Gideon and his innuendo which might mean nothing at all, and might mean that the police were after him for the five-year-old crime, and he kept wondering where Jane was. If the police ever found and questioned her, what would she do?

He could no longer even contemplate Charlotte's murder, yet he was in desperate need of Clare.

God dammit, it wasn't possible that the police . . .

Wasn't it? he kept asking himself tensely. Was he trying to fool himself—the man who boasted that no one could fool him? Would any man in authority at Scotland Yard talk as Gideon had for the sake of it? What should he do if the police were trying to build up a charge?

Ought he to consult his lawyers? Wouldn't it be better if they could brief him now, advising him exactly what to do and say if the police did act? Should he tell them about Jane Kennett, and ask for their legal guidance?

Could he *blame* Jane, if the police did suspect?

He reached the Madeleine, stood at the foot of the wide stone steps topped by the great columns, then went up them slowly, and into the shadowy depths of the church; but he found no peace, because he could not make up his mind what he ought to do.

* * * * *

Reggie Cole's mother could not make up her mind what to do, either.

She knew that something was badly wrong with her son, though she had no idea what, and whenever she broached the subject he would get up and go out, or turn on the television loudly, or tell her that it was none of her business, that he was backing the winners. He was often out later at night than ever before, too, he was completely unpredictable, and he no longer pretended that he was going to see a film.

It was now half past five, and he would be home at any time. Almost at that moment she heard him at the front door, and was in the kitchen when he entered the passage. He moved softly, as if anxious that she should not know that he was there; he often did that these days. He had come to put on his best suit, of course; he dressed up most evenings. She heard him creep along to his small room and, a few minutes later, heard the bathroom door click to.

Mrs Cole slipped out of the kitchen and went into Reggie's room. His working clothes were hanging over a chair, the trousers in a heap, but she ignored the familiar untidiness and picked up his coat. His wallet wasn't in it. She looked round, and caught a glimpse of her reflection in the mirror; she was a small, thin-featured woman, rather flat-breasted, and with a harassed expression; and just now she was more harassed than ever. She felt under the pillow of Reggie's bed but his wallet wasn't there, looked into the two drawers of a small, whitewood dressing-table, stood for a moment in doubt and misgivings, and then lifted up the foot of the mattress.

There was the wallet; fat with notes.

She snatched it up, took the notes out, and counted them hurriedly, muttering each numeral under her breath. There were three five-pound and a lot of one-pound notes.

". . . thirteen, fourteen, fifteen, sixteen, seventeen, eighteen," she breathed.

So he had thirty-three pounds which he was trying to hide from her, yet he earned only six pounds a week; here were six weeks' wages! Moreover, he was spending money freely, on cigarettes, on new shirts and socks and ties.

"I've got to have it out with him," she told herself, but she was almost frightened because of the way he had behaved of late, and because she did not want to drive him away from her. If she quarrelled with him, he might never confide in her again; and the day might come when he would need her help desperately. That was why she had said nothing to his father, who would insist on 'having it out'.

She heard the bathroom door open and hesitated, in great distress of mind. She could put the wallet back and pretend she had come in for some trifle, or she could stand and face her son. All her life she had been putting off unpleasant duties, and all her life she had suffered for her lack of resolution.

She set her teeth, and stood with the bulky wallet in her hand. Reggie came in, hurrying, wearing only his pants and a vest. He pulled up short, and for a moment he seemed horrified at sight of her; he was the small boy of a few years ago, the baby of loved memory. In that moment, his mother thought that she might be able to reach him with understanding, and she tried to make her voice sound gentle, without knowing that in fact she sounded ingratiating.

"Reggie, dear, isn't this rather a lot of money?"

"Mother, *dear*," he said, after a kind of gasp. "That's a hell of a lot of money, and it happens to be mine." He came forward and snatched the wallet away. "What do you mean by coming in here and sneaking about my room?"

Desperately his mother went on trying:

"Reggie, I'm worried about you, dear. When you're young you don't always understand the dangers of bad company and–and betting, and—"

"I understand that I can live my own life, and I've every right to," Reggie said roughly. "If I can't call this room my own and be sure you won't go prying about it, I can find plenty of bigger and better rooms. You'd better make up your mind whether you want me at home or not."

She felt as if her head would burst.

"Reggie, I–I'm only trying to help you. You're my own flesh and blood, and—"

"Your own flesh and blood's got a date, and he's going to keep it," Reggie said, and he sounded almost vicious. She was more fearful than ever that if she insisted on an explanation she would be driving him from his own home. She could never do it; she would have to be patient, and await her chance. She would really have to talk it over with his father soon . . .

CHAPTER 10

ARREST

"WHO'S GOING to make the arrest?" Bell asked.

He knew that there was nothing that Gideon would rather do, but that the actual duty of charging Borgman had to be delegated. That was one of the disadvantages of being Commander. Gideon did not reply immediately, for he was looking through the final report which had just been returned by the Public Prosecutor's office with a laconic: '*Recommendation agreed.*' There was no doubt that the finding of the hidden store of morphine solution had been the deciding factor. Add that to the autopsy report, and there was no possible doubt that they had a case. Gideon was thinking that his original plan, to concentrate on the accident method and then to switch to the morphine, would have to be dropped. In the desk at Borgman's office there was everything needed to clinch a straightforward charge of murdering his wife by poisoning. If only that nurse . . .

"What's that?" he asked.

"Who's going to make the arrest?" Bell repeated.

"Freddy, of course, and Carmichael will be with him," Gideon answered. "Might be a good idea to have Jim Appleby there, too, while the office is being searched." He turned back to his own report and recommendations, trying to make sure that he had not slipped up; and a telephone bell rang. Automatically, he lifted it. "Gideon . . . Right, thanks." He rang off, and his voice was very strong. "Borgman's on his way from London Airport. He'll be at his office in three-quarters of an hour."

"Why don't you go yourself? A big man is involved."

"Forget it." Gideon lifted a telephone, and said: "Give me Mr Lee." He held on. Lee answered almost at once, and Gideon gave the instructions.

"Okay, it will be a pleasure," Lee said, and obviously

his satisfaction remained, so nothing had yet affected his new-found confidence. "There's something queer about that bottle of morphine at the back of my mind," he added.

"You've had it checked by the manufacturers, haven't you?"

"Oh, yes. No doubt what it is. I can't find out how Borgman got it, though. I'd be happier if I could."

"Tried all the chemists he used to know?"

"All I can trace," Lee said, and then went on briskly: "I'll keep at it—might as well get as many nails for his coffin as we can."

"I couldn't agree more," Gideon said. "Right, Fred." He rang off, and immediately called Appleby, and told him to be with Lee. Now that the moment had come, he was edgy, worried that in spite of the final evidence, there might be a snag which he had not seen. No one else seemed to have noticed one; Lee's wasn't really a snag. He forced himself to think of other jobs, and studied a report from the laboratory about the Japanese gloves found in a garage in New King's Road, Fulham. "I'm going up to see Sammy," he announced, and went out, letting the door swing to behind him. Five minutes later he was in the long, narrow room where most of the forensic work of the Yard was done. There were five white-smocked assistants at the long bench, and he recognised two blood tests being made, under microscopes, saw the remains of a human hand lying on a sheet of blotting paper, some tufts of hair torn out of a woman's head in a fight with a drunk, and several other exhibits which he did not recognise. Sammy, or Dr Samuel Griddle, the country's leading pathologist, was a short man standing by a stool which had the odd effect of making him seem very small, poking at something on a sheet of white paper. He had very thick-lensed glasses.

"What's that you've got there?" Gideon asked.

"Hallo, George. Can't you see?"

"Hairs," Gideon said, knowing that was exactly what Sammy wanted him to say.

Sammy stopped poking at the curly hairs, looked up at him, and echoed:

"Hairs. How you can stand there and say it, I don't know. What kind of hair? Human? Dog's? Horse's? Pig's? If human, what sex? If male, from what part? Head? Nape of neck? Ears? Nostrils? Armpits? Arms, hands, legs—"

"Masculine pubic hairs," Gideon said, straight-faced.

"Glad you haven't lost all sense of observation," said Sammy, and gave a smirk of a grin. "You're right for once. Not that it's funny, though. Male pubic hairs which we're trying to match up with that assault on Mary Cunliffe."

Mary Cunliffe was a seven-year-old child.

Gideon said: "Oh, God. Why do they?" For a few moments thought of Borgman was driven from his mind, and he saw the picture which lay behind this slip of white paper and these few greying hairs. A family in despair; wife, mother, father and three older children. A seven-year-old, assaulted and strangled. The wife of an old man prostrate with horror lest it be proved that her husband had committed this hideous crime.

Sammy said: "You always did take these things badly, George, didn't you. What have you come for?"

"That Japanese cotton glove."

"Over here," said Sammy, and moved towards another spot on the long bench beneath a wide window. There were the gloves, each in a separate plastic container, and the strands which had led to their discovery. Attached to them all was a typewritten report, which was the evidence that Sammy, or one of his assistants, would give in court when the time came, proving beyond doubt that these particular strands had come from that particular glove. The blood group—'A'—was the same, and there was a magnified photograph showing how strands of cotton had been cut by the glass and the jagged edge; multiplied a hundred times it showed the fracture clearly.

"Satisfied?" Sammy asked.

"Nearly. Did you have Larkin's clothes up here?"

"Yes."

"Nail scraping?"

"Yes."

"Photographs?"

"Yes," said Sammy, and pulled open a drawer, in which were a man's clothes, all neatly folded, each one with a ticket attached and a report typewritten inside a plastic envelope. There was a pair of rubber-soled brown shoes, a pair of red and blue socks, a handkerchief. "Haven't finished the analysis of the dust taken from the clothes yet—no hurry with this one, is there?"

Gideon was studying the photograph.

"I should think so. Bandaged right hand—and we've a blood-stained right-hand cotton glove."

"Well, I'm damned," said Sammy, and took off his glasses and wiped his eyes. "You seen this before?"

"Read a report from QR Division that this chap had been found battered to death, and that he had a bandaged right hand," said Gideon, "and I just wanted to make sure."

Sammy called across to one of the white-clad assistants: "Walter! Got the dust analysis on the new corpus yet?"

"Coming up."

"Done the shoes?" asked Gideon.

"Yes, sir. Traces of heavy grease of the kind used for greasing nipples and chassis parts of motor cars, particles of oily dust likely to have come from a garage. Finger-nails normal."

"Where's the body?" asked Gideon.

"In the morgue at QR."

"Will you send someone over to check that hand wound; you might find a strand of this Jap cotton in it," Gideon said. "If this is the chap who stole that car and ran down the man and the youngster, we're really up against something."

"I never did like the kill-to-keep-'em-quiet cases," Sammy remarked, and rubbed his eyes again, looking troubled. "Walter, you can go over to QR, can't you?"

"Yes, sir."

"Well, then, don't hang about." Sammy looked up at Gideon and asked: "Think you've really got Borgman?"

"Wouldn't pull him in if I didn't," Gideon answered, and he was aware that all the assistants were glancing at him, and that Sammy was more intent than usual. Borgman had this effect. Gideon had seldom said anything about it, but practically everyone at the Yard knew what he thought about Borgman, and knew how much he wanted to make the murder charge stick. They were not yet convinced that the charge would stick. Here in the laboratory everything had to be checked and double-checked; they dare not risk being confuted by experts, and chemical facts were chemical facts. Gideon had little unassailable evidence. The whole Yard knew what he had got, and while there was a sense of jubilation in many, there was also an edge of doubt. Borgman was big: Borgman would fight back: there would be another battle royal with Percy Richmond.

Gideon felt almost as if he himself were to be put on trial.

He sensed it as he walked down the stairs, preferring to do that rather than take the lift. He had been in the laboratory for half an hour, so Borgman would be at his office, and might by now be under arrest; might be on his way here. Gideon reached his own floor level, and went slowly and deliberately to the door; but for once he hesitated before he opened it. One ugly question was in his mind; could he really be sure about Borgman? Not that he had murdered his wife, but that the crime could be proved against him. Had Fred Lee's memory teased him because of subconscious doubt? Was there any way to prove that Borgman had obtained that morphine himself? Why couldn't they find that nurse?

As he went in, two telephone bells rang at once. He strode to his desk for one while Bell lifted the other. He heard Bell say: "Commander Gideon's office," and then heard the operator say:

"Mr Appleby on the line, sir."

"Put him on."

There was a longer pause than he had expected; the kind of pause which might come if Appleby had bad news. What could have gone wrong? Why hadn't he cut red tape and gone over himself?

"George?"

"How'd it go?"

"Easy as kiss your hand," Appleby said. "Ever heard the old story of the man who went white to the lips?" Appleby's chuckle had an almost cruel note. "Green *and* white, Borgman went. Fred's bringing him over now; he'll be with you in twenty minutes."

"Find the morphine?" Gideon fought against being too jubilant.

"You'd never believe, it was hidden in a secret compartment in his desk! Mr Borgman says that he'd never seen it before; isn't that a funny story? Okay, George, thought I'd put you out of your misery."

"Thanks," said Gideon.

Well, he had got his way. He felt a little flushed as he rounded his desk and sat down. He had been after Borgman for so long and it was hard to believe that he had him. He had a swift mental pre-view of the next few weeks, perhaps the next few months. The magistrate's court tomorrow, and the formal charge and request for a remand; that would be almost automatic. The court would be jammed with newspapermen, and half of social Mayfair would want to get into the tiny public gallery. Outside there would be hundreds of people, all gawpers, waiting to gloat over the mighty fallen. Then there would be the eight furious days while Borgman was in Brixton, spending most of the time with his solicitors and Richmond—he was bound to brief Richmond, wasn't he?—while Gideon, Fred Lee and Carmichael were getting a cast-iron case ready for the second hearing.

"I want him sent for trial by then," Gideon said to himself. "If we miss, we might wait until after Christmas."

The door opened, and Rogerson looked in.

"Got him?"

"Yes."

"Keep your fingers crossed," Rogerson said.

The truth was that no one felt really confident, in spite of the weight of the evidence; there would be that edge of doubt until the jury had returned their verdict. There was just one witness who might take away that doubt. Gideon flipped over the file on the Borgman case, and saw a new report, put there since he had last opened it. He could hardly believe the terse teleprinted message.

> 'Nurse Jane Kennett married Piet Hoorn Fremantle Western Australia February 16th 1957 STOP Hoorn died December 1959 natural causes STOP Widow known to have flown London January 7th this year Qantas Airways STOP Delaney Criminal Investigation Bureau Perth Western Australia.'

"My God!" Gideon breathed, and snatched at a telephone, then saw a pencilled slip which had fallen from the file. Joe Bell had written: 'Am checking Qantas passenger list January 7th. It's all under way.'

Gideon said: "Well, well, well. She's been in England."

Then he wondered if she had seen Borgman, but before he could develop that train of thought, a telephone bell rang. It was Colby, of AB Division.

"Hallo, George. You asked me to tell you who it was found those gloves at Bennett's Garage."

"Yes."

"It was Detective Sergeant Willerby."

"I'd like a word with him some time—when's he going to be in?" Gideon asked, knowing that Colby hadn't called up about this.

"All afternoon," said Colby. "Come and have a cuppa." Then he added in the same breath: "I hear you're picking up Borgman at last."

"We've got him, Ken."

"Hope so," said Colby. "I—oh, hell, the blasted telephone never keeps quiet. See you." He rang off, and

Gideon found himself momentarily on the edge of doubt again. He made a note to be at Colby's headquarters just after four o'clock, then telephoned the Guildford police, where the sergeant who had caught Carslake was stationed. He had to keep busy. A word with the man's C.O. might do a lot of good, a pat on the back for the sergeant even more.

"Gideon here," he said. "How's that chap Miles, who got Carslake? Didn't he hurt his hand?"

"Only a scratch," said the Guildford man. "Nice of you to ring, Mr Gideon."

"Damned plucky job, from all accounts, and we wanted Carslake badly. Ask Miles to look in here any time he's in town, I'd like to go over one or two things in his report."

"Be sure I will."

"Good," said Gideon, and then saw the door open and half expected Borgman; but instead it was Appleby. Of course he would be warned in good time; no one would bring Borgman here unannounced; the whole case was putting him off balance.

Appleby looked on top of the world, bright, eager, like an excited turkey.

"Ready for him, George? He's downstairs."

"Bring him up," said Gideon.

CHAPTER II

FIRST HEARING

GIDEON HAD a telephone at his ear, but no one at the end of it, when the door opened and Borgman stepped in. Gideon glanced up at him, and his first impression was disappointing; whatever Borgman had felt like at the moment of the charge, he was composed now; except that he was tight-lipped, he looked the same as at his last visit. Gideon kept him there while first Appleby and then Lee and Bell came in, Lee carrying a small case. In that case would be the morphine and the hypodermic needles found in the desk.

"All right, call me as soon as you've got the date for the trial," Gideon said, then put down the receiver and looked up. He made no attempt to stand, stared for what must have seemed a long time to Borgman, and then said: "Well, Mr Borgman?"

Borgman said, without heat or emotion: "I have already told your men that this charge is ludicrous. I have nothing more to say until I have been able to consult my lawyers."

"You're at liberty to consult them whenever you like," Gideon said. "But we don't waste our time, Mr Borgman, and we don't make serious charges unless we can support them."

"There are not the slightest grounds for this charge," Borgman insisted. His voice was still flat, but the anger was in his eyes. It was obvious that he had got himself under a strict control; that he was making sure that he did not say a word that might increase his danger.

"I see," said Gideon. "What did you find in Mr Borgman's office, Superintendent?"

Lee was already opening his case, and without a word he took out two hypodermic syringes and a small bottle of morphine solution—or what looked like morphine and was marked morphine; but there was always the outside possibility that it was a harmless liquid. Lee had tasted it, but could he be really positive?

"I have never seen those things before," Borgman said, gratingly now.

Gideon raised his eyebrows.

"Really, Mr Borgman?"

"I've told you—" Borgman stopped, moistened his lips, and then said: "I have nothing more to say."

"Very well, Mr Borgman. You will be lodged in a cell at Cannon Row police station, close by here, for the night, and the formal first hearing will be heard in the morning. If there is anything you want we will provide it, within reason. You may have special food brought in if you wish it, although no alcohol. You may have cigarettes." Gideon glanced at Appleby. "Will you take him away, Mr Appleby, please?"

Borgman burst out: "You must be mad."

"I don't feel particularly abnormal," Gideon retorted mildly, and Appleby took Borgman's arm and led him to the door. They went out. As the door closed, Bell was smiling, and Lee grinning.

"Fred, take this stuff up to Sammy," Gideon said urgently. "Stand over him while he analyses it; we want to be a hundred per cent certain that it's what we think it is. Any prints on it?"

"Haven't checked yet," Lee said. "They might have been wiped off, anyhow; it's nothing to worry about."

"That's the trouble, the vision of getting Borgman is making us careless," Gideon said. "It's almost as if the case has got a blight. No, I'm only joking, Fred. You remembered what was puzzling you about the bottles?"

"No." Lee was already putting the tiny bottles and the hypodermic needles back in his case, and the startled look was still in his eyes. "But I will." He went out, and Gideon said:

"Any news of that nurse?"

"She arrived on January 12th after a couple of stop-overs, then went on a European coach tour organised by

Thomas Cook's," Bell said. "I've just had word. But that's as far as we go. She ended the tour in Paris, six weeks ago. I'm checking all airlines and all shipping lines to try to find out if she left the country, and I've sent a call out to all British police forces, asking them to check hotels."

"Fine," said Gideon.

"I want him just as badly as you do," Bell said. "I'm beginning—"

He broke off as one of Gideon's telephones rang. It might be from any one of a thousand people and about any one of a thousand cases, but Gideon did not think it was, and he was almost relieved when he heard Rogerson's voice. Rogerson was quite back to normal, and in his way seemed as excited as anyone.

"George, I'm told he's here."

"I've sent him across the road."

"Be careful with him," Rogerson urged. "If we even gave him an accidental shove, it would be built up by his counsel into criminal assault. Cuthbertson had been on to me already, and he'll be here in twenty minutes. I think you'd better handle him; don't leave it to one of the others."

"I'll handle him," Gideon promised. "We've got a line on that nurse," he added. He was grinning.

"George," said Rogerson, "I take back all I said."

But it was not a thing to grin about; it would be tough. Cuthbertson, of Cuthbertson, Foyle and Cuthbertson, was one of the most astute lawyers in London, and he had prepared a dozen cases for Percy Richmond. The shape of things to come was already clear, and it was developing rapidly. There had been little time, but someone was already working hard for Borgman, knowing who to send for, and what to do. It wasn't likely to be his wife, for it was doubtful whether she had heard of the arrest yet. When she did, it would be a bad shock, but—he could forget Borgman's present wife; he had to remember only that he had started the chain of events, and had to see it through to the end.

What the hell was it that Lee couldn't remember?

When would that woman be traced?

* * * * *

Cuthbertson was a man of medium height, silvery-haired, gentle-voiced. He was not yet sixty, although his strangely pink and white skin and his gentleness sometimes suggested that he was a much older man. He knew Gideon well. He had briefed Percy Richmond when the Yard had lost that first big case. He knew exactly what kind of struggle lay ahead, yet was as pleasant and charming as if he had come in to pass the time of day.

"I know you will give Mr Borgman all the customary facilities," he said, "and I know you'll be the first to apologise when you realise what a grotesque mistake has been made." He smiled. "I would like to see Mr Borgman alone as soon as possible, of course."

"I'll fix it," Gideon said, and then asked as if gruffly: "Did his secretary send for you?"

"Yes."

"From London, or from Paris?"

"I don't quite understand you," Cuthbertson said, quite amiably. "She telephoned me from the London office, of course—very properly, too. Clare Selby is a most efficient young woman."

"Take Mr Cuthbertson across to the prisoner," Gideon said stonily.

When he was alone in the office, he got up and stood by the window, looking on to the sunlit Thames, seeing the fast-moving traffic, seeing the slender dignity of the tower of Big Ben. He would be uneasy until the verdict had been given, and that was a long way ahead. Why didn't Lee come back with the analyst's report? Surely Sammy could make a rough test to make sure—

A telephone bell rang.

"Gideon."

"You're safe so far, George," said Sammy. "This stuff is morphine all right, and there's powdered morphia in the little box, too. Anyone with access to that stuff could have killed a whole family. But there's one thing you'd prefer to have different."

"What's that?"

"Not a fingerprint of any kind on needle, syringe, bottle or box," Sammy said. "Lee's gone down to Fingerprints to check, but you can take it from me that you won't be able to prove that Borgman handled that bottle. You'll have to rely on circumstantial evidence for that."

Gideon grunted. "Hm." He was thinking, and Sammy was thinking, that Richmond would almost certainly deny that Borgman had put the poisons and the instruments in that desk. But that shouldn't be hard to establish, and in any case the amount of the poison in the remains of the body should clinch the issue. He said: "Thanks, Sam," and rang off. Two calls came in about new jobs, just reported; a factory robbery of expensive machine tools, and the theft of a truck load of cigarettes. That was going to hit the headlines. He wrenched his mind off Borgman, telephoned Records, and was answered by a man with a perky voice.

"Smith here."

"Smithy, haven't we sent you down more inquiries about factory jobs than usual?"

"Could be," said Chief Inspector Smith.

"Check, will you?" asked Gideon. "There's another small tools job out on the Great West Road, not big, but enough to worry about if it's being organised."

"Can't find a market for small tools like you can for furs or jewels," Smith argued.

"So far as we know," Gideon said, and rang off, thinking about how often men said the obvious, and wondering how often he did. He made notes about several factory thefts which had been reported lately; then Bell came in.

"Greeted each other like long-lost brothers," he said, and he sounded a little uneasy. "I never liked the smooth type, and Cuthbertson's smoother than most." He went to his chair. "Anything new in?"

"No. Take all the calls for the next hour, will you?

I want another go at these car thefts, and I want to check the build-up against the Carters."

"You've got them as tight as a glove," said Bell, and gave Gideon the impression that he had been going to add: 'Wish you had Borgman as tight.' Gideon pushed the thought aside, but it kept coming back. He wished he knew what was going on between the man and his solicitor, and it was not even a consolation to know that the case against Red and Syd Carter was fool-proof. He rang Plumley, who said brightly:

"Nice job you've done about the Carters, George. Wish all cases were as easy as that."

"You call it easy?" Gideon said gruffly. "About to-morrow morning—I've got Lee to give evidence of arrest, and Carmichael and Appleby to support. Do you want to give any other evidence?"

Plumley hesitated.

"Cuthbertson will probably put up a show of outraged innocence," Gideon went on, "but I don't think we ought to show even a glimpse of our cards."

"Right, George. We'll just give formal evidence and let them snarl."

"Good," said Gideon.

* * * * *

Waiting seldom worried Gideon, for he had learned patience the hard way. Sometimes weeks, often months, occasionally years, passed before he got what evidence he needed, and he had a sense of timelessness most of the time he was at the Yard. He could act as swiftly as any man, but the slow accretion of evidence satisfied him best. At the moment there were a dozen, perhaps twice as many, men out, patiently acquiring evidence: about the car thefts, for instance; about the factory thefts; about the Carters; about the old lecher; about Carslake and Mrs Robson. Remorselessly, cases built up. But waiting that night was more trying than he had known it for a long time. He took the robbery files home, as well as notes about the factory jobs and the file on the man Larkin who had been battered to death in a small room of a house where he had lived with his mother and father. It began to look very much as if Larkin had driven that killer car—and been killed so that he could not talk.

Usually, the telephone bell would ring two or three times in an evening, especially when O'Leary was on duty. Tonight, it did not ring once. Kate had to go out, sitting in for a neighbour. The television palled. It was useless to tell himself that he was fussing like a hen: this was how he felt.

At ten o'clock the children began to come in. Malcolm was full of a film he had just seen, Matthew was in a lively mood, Penelope and Priscilla had a fit of the giggles. After ten minutes, Gideon said: "I'm going out for a stroll," and went off, wishing Kate were with him, wishing that he was more sure of himself, looking up at the stars without thinking about them. He heard footsteps coming round the corner, and recognised Kate's. There was more spring in his step as he went to meet her. The light of a street lamp fell on her face, and he saw her smile as she recognised him.

"Hallo, Kate. You're early."

"I wanted to be," Kate said, as they touched hands. "Is Malcolm home?"

"They're all in. It's a bear garden," Gideon said. "Care for a stroll?"

"Love it."

"Let's go to the river," Gideon suggested. "Bus there and walk back."

"That's a good idea," agreed Kate.

She was aware of his mood, of course, even though she did not speak of it, and there was the quietness of true companionship between them as they walked to New King's Road, caught a bus after only a minute's wait, went to the Middlesex side of Putney Bridge, and walked briskly over it. The stars were reflected brightly on a surface so calm that there seemed to be hardly any movement. No craft was on it, only a few lights showed near the water, but the lights of the bridge shimmered just inside. A police car swung towards them, travelling very fast. They walked with long, well-matched strides, down to the tow-path, along it for half a mile, and then back, gradually quickening their pace; and when they reached the house again Gideon was feeling practically normal. Malcolm and the girls had gone to bed, Matthew was studying at a corner of the kitchen table, with the radio on. A supper tray with tea and sandwiches was waiting for them, and Kate said:

"Going to be long, Matt?"

"Only half an hour. I can go up to my room, if you like."

"You stay here, we'll go up to our room," Kate said.

That was just right, thought Gideon, just what he wanted.

* * * * *

Next morning, when he kissed her lightly, Kate squeezed his hand and said:

"Good luck, dear."

* * * * *

Gideon stood in the magistrate's court at Marlborough Street, the biggest man present. A court that was often almost deserted was bursting at the seams. Newspaper men squeezed together so that three sat where there was comfortable room for one, for they regarded this as the biggest sensation of the year. The morning's papers had headlined the arrest, even *The Times* had given it prominence. Lee and Sergeant Carmichael were waiting, Carmichael rather like Cuthbertson to look at, with a distinguished profile and greying hair, Lee impervious to everything but his notes; he was undoubtedly feeling very much on edge.

Gideon looked round at the public gallery, and saw Mrs Borgman at the end of one row with Foyle, the junior partner of the solicitors. She was a striking woman, probably in the early forties, and obviously she had been a real beauty, but now she was a little too fat and heavy-breasted. But her complexion was superb, and as she looked about the court he saw that she had the most beautiful dark eyes. At the other end of the same bench was a slim blonde, a real beauty, and there was no reasonable doubt that this was Clare Selby. Gideon wondered whether Borgman's wife knew that her husband had spent the weekend in Paris with the girl, who could only be in the middle twenties. She had an air of competence and poise, looking more like a model than a secretary.

The clerk to the court came in, a wisp of a man, grey, dark-clad, harassed-looking, wearing *pince-nez*; off duty, he was one of the best raconteurs Gideon knew, with a store of court lore that wasn't bettered in all London. Then a police sergeant banged his gavel, intoned words which were indistinguishable, and everyone stood up; Gideon saw how easily the Selby girl rose, and noticed that Borgman's wife made quite an effort of it, like many heavy women. She was surprisingly short, when standing, and looked almost dumpy, as many Italian and Jewish women did after the first years of their womanhood.

The magistrate came in: Calahan, a newly appointed one, with a brisk air and so far as the police were concerned an unknown quantity.

Then Borgman was called.

Gideon sensed the tension in the public and the Press gallery, but the rest was so matter-of-fact that it was almost boring. Yet when Borgman came in, immaculate in navy blue, brisk-moving, touched with dignity, Gideon felt that old familiar feeling of edginess. There was no further news of the nurse, and he was keenly disappointed. Then he saw Borgman look across at his wife and smile; the smile softened his expression remarkably, and made an immediate appeal to the people in the court. His wife raised both hands, as if she longed to cross to him and take him in her arms.

Lee was called.

"Do I understand that it is your intention only to submit evidence of arrest?" the magistrate asked.

"Yes, sir."

"Please proceed." The formality was absurd, and yet it bristled with drama, because of the accused man and the way he was looking at his wife. Gideon watched the blonde, and could not say that she took any more notice of Borgman than anyone else did. Her lips were parted a fraction, as if she were touched by the prevailing excitement.

". . . and we ask for time in which to prepare the evidence against the accused," said Lee.

"I understand," said Calahan.

Was he going to be a prosy fool?

"Is the accused represented?"

"Yes, your worship," Cuthbertson said, and stood up.

"Thank you. Does the accused wish to say anything?"

"I am not guilty, sir," Borgman said.

"My client will have a complete answer to the charge laid against him," said Cuthbertson, "and in view of his great responsibilities in public life, and the fact that the charge refers to a matter nearly five years old, I respectfully submit that bail on any recognisances which you see fit to impose would be far more just than a remand in custody."

"Hmm-hmm-mm," said Calahan, and Gideon watched him with increasing tension; was there any possible risk that he would agree? It *could* happen; Borgman could put up a huge bond.

"Hmm-mmm-mm," Calahan said again. "In view of the gravity of the charge, I do not think it advisable to order a remand on bail. Eight days in custody—where every facility will be given to the defence, of course, every facility—is that what you require, Superintendent?"

"That will be satisfactory, your Worship."

"Very well," said Calahan. "The accused will appear again in this court on Wednesday next." He paused, Cuthbertson touched Borgman's arm, Mrs Borgman pushed her way towards the box and no one stopped her from greeting her husband, while Clare Selby looked on as if dispassionately.

Outside, Lee said: "Calahan had me scared for a minute."

"Now I'm going to scare you," Gideon said. "You've got more work to do in the next week than you've ever done in your life. We mustn't miss a trick, and if we can prove Borgman obtained that morphine himself, or even had the opportunity to, we'll clinch it even tighter. I'll spend the afternoon with you on the job. Okay?"

"I won't miss any tricks," Lee said fervently, and his mouth was set thinly. "I want to win this case even more than you do, George."

There were times when it would have been an advantage to be back as a superintendent, Gideon reflected, as he was driven to the Yard by a plainclothes sergeant who thought it was advisable not to talk. He could then tackle one job at a time, as Lee did. The moment he got back he would find a dozen jobs waiting for him, and good though Joe Bell was, there was a limit to how much he could take on himself. He hurried to the office, and found Bell on the telephone. Gideon glanced through the notes on his desk, and one of them read:

'*I've told D. I. Wills to be here at twelve—he's got something on the killer car job.*'

It was now half past eleven.

Bell rang off, made a note, and asked: "Everything as you wanted it?" He hardly waited for an answer, but went on: "Nasty job in this morning."

"What?"

"Six-year-old girl who was missing last night found strangled near the spot where the seven-year-old was three nights ago."

Gideon said: "But that old man—"

"It wasn't him, George. Sammy rang down to say those hairs weren't his, anyhow."

Gideon said: "Damn," and lifted the telephone. "Give me the laboratory: I'll hold on." He waited for ten seconds, and then said: "Sammy there? . . . Sammy, the pubic hairs in that seven-year old's knickers, were they the same as the specimens you had this morning? . . . Oh. Sure? . . . Right . . . Yes, carry on . . . Really?" His tone brightened. "Looks as if we're really all right there, anyhow." He rang off. "As it wasn't the old man they arrested in B.1, we'd better make sure he's released with full apologies." He lifted the telephone again. "Get me Mr Summerley of B.1, quick." He rang off. "But Sammy says that they've found strands from that cotton glove in the pocket of the man Larkin; he did that job all right. Did we pick up the manager of that garage where we found the gloves?"

"That's what Wills wants to see you about."

"Right." A telephone bell rang, and Gideon picked it up. "Thanks . . . that you, Summerley? . . . That old man for the seven-year-old child job—oh, you have—good. Hope to God they catch the swine who really did it, soon. Good-bye."

He picked up a memo with Bell's initials appended, and read:

'Mrs Jane Hoorn travelled by P. & O. Line to Bombay, India, on the R.M.S. *Himla*, March 5th. She had a short sight-sceing trip in Bombay and Southern India. The P. & O. Line is trying to trace her beyond that. I have cabled Bombay Police Department.'

Gideon said very softly:

"Nice work, Joe. We'll get her before long." Before he could go on, his telephone bell rang again.

"It won't give me a minute's peace this morning," he said irritably, and picked up the receiver, prepared to switch his thoughts right away from Borgman. "Gideon . . . Who? . . . Yes, put him through." He raised a hand to Bell, who immediately picked up an extension of the same telephone, and a pencil. "It's Limpy Dale," he called, a hand covering the mouthpiece. "Might be a squeal on the Carters . . . Hallo, Dale, yes—Gideon speaking. Will you—"

"Mr. Gideon, I've only got sec," a man began, but abruptly his voice broke off, there was a sound which might have been a stifled cry, then silence until the line at the other end went dead, creating an awful stillness.

That was one of the bad moments for Gideon; a moment when the men against whom he was working seemed to stretch out to hit him where he sat.

The Carters were in a prison cell; but someone working for them must have stopped Limpy, and there seemed only one possible explanation of that stifled cry.

CHAPTER 12

BAD DAY

"He was going to squeak all right," Joe Bell said, "and they stopped him, George." He watched as Gideon rattled the platform of the telephone, and as Gideon said into it: "Get me Mr Christy, in a hurry." Gideon didn't replace his receiver, but called to Bell: "Get Information, Joe. We want a general call out for Limpy Dale as fast as we can get it." Bell snatched up a telephone, and there was a few moments' delay. During them he felt the same kind of shock as Gideon had, and wished he could take a few minutes off, to absorb the news; but Gideon seemed like perpetual motion when there was any kind of emergency such as this.

"Ask the riverside Divisions to concentrate on this, and have the Thames Division watch the river; there's a chance that they'll throw him in," he said to Bell. "Hallo, Hugh, here's an emergency. Limpy Dale was going to squeal but I think someone stopped him. We want to pick him up as fast as we can. I've a general call out, but will you . . . Good man." Christy had told him that he was already ringing for a sergeant to arrange calls at places where Limpy Dale might be found. "Call me in person," Gideon urged. "No, I don't know what he was going to squeal about, he didn't have time to say."

He rang off, listened to Bell talking to Information, and then looked up as there was a tap at the door. "Come in." The door opened and Detective-Inspector Wills came in, a youngish man with a lean, powerful figure; Wills was thirty-eight, and would go a long way. "Sit down a minute, Wills," Gideon said as Bell finished talking. "Joe, there are two things to concentrate on with Limpy Dale. Either he was going to turn Queen's Evidence, and so try to save his own skin, or he was going to tell us something we don't know. If it had been Queen's

Evidence he would have written to us, I should think, or said something to Christy's boys when he was questioned. So it looks as if there's something brewing."

"Can't think what, as we've got both Red and Syd."

"That's what worries me," Gideon said. "There's one obvious possibility." He glanced round at Wills, gave a thin-lipped smile, and said: "Care to guess what it is?"

Wills had a deep voice and a friendly smile.

"Couldn't be a plan to get Red and Syd Carter out of Brixton, could it?"

Gideon smiled broadly. "It's the kind of thing I think we ought to watch for, anyhow." It was good to know that Wills was on the ball so quickly, to have confirmation that here was a man with a real future. "Well, what's worrying you about Bennett, the manager of that garage? Picked him up?"

"No," answered Wills, and where another man might have seemed diffident, he was confident without being in any way over-bold. "That's what I wanted a word with you about, sir. The gloves were in his wastepaper basket, and we've got grounds for picking him up, but I shouldn't think he's a talker. I'd prefer to let him think we accept his explanation that he didn't know the gloves were there, and hadn't seen Larkin."

"What do you know about Larkin?"

"Just been talking to the lab, sir," Wills replied. "I had seen a report about his murder, of course, and he had a bandaged right hand, so I wondered if there could be a connection."

"Hm. How would you handle the situation?"

"I'd let Bennett have reason to believe we're going to ask him about Larkin, so that he can prepare himself against the question," Wills said, "and I'd let him get away with a denial that he saw Larkin yesterday. That will encourage Bennett to think he's safe, and he might do something he wouldn't risk if he was on his guard."

"Why not come straight out with it, and try to make him break down?"

"As I say, he doesn't strike me as a man who'll break

easily, sir, and there are no sign of Bennett's prints at Larkin's place," answered Wills. "I've discovered something else about Bennett, sir."

"What?"

"He nearly went broke a year ago, and then got some new capital in his business. Since then he's been spending pretty freely. I had a look at his takings books, and I shouldn't think he's doing much business. I've also discovered that several garages which were a bit rocky last year are doing all right now—these little one-man garages, run by the boss and a boy. There are at least five of that kind of garage in the South-West London area, and they've all taken on a new lease of life."

"All right, lay off Bennett for the time being. Anything else?"

"I'd suggest having a man at one of the other garages, possibly one each at a couple of them," Wills said. "We could get a couple of young-looking chaps with good mechanical knowledge, and they might pick up a lot. I don't think you'll get much luck at Bennett's, but there's no reason why the others shouldn't bite."

"Got the men in mind?"

"There's a chap named Arthurson in the Mechanics School, sir," Wills said. "Apart from that I'm pretty blank."

"I'll talk to the Mechanics Superintendent, and tell him you'll be getting in touch," said Gideon. "Think you can handle this yourself, or would you rather have a superintendent with you?"

Wills just grinned.

Gideon chuckled. "See what you can do." He nodded dismissal, and when Wills was opening the door, said: "Oh, Wills."

Wills turned. "Yes, sir?"

"Don't take chances. These chaps are killers. And don't make mistakes. If you're in doubt, come to me or Mr Bell. There's a lot of things you haven't had time to learn yet. A bad mistake now could keep you back from promotion for years."

"I'll watch my step, sir."

"Good luck," said Gideon. He waited until the door had closed, and then grinned across at Bell. "Watch him, Joe. He might want taking down a peg, or two soon; we'll have to judge the moment right. He may be on to the very thing we're after, too; if these garages are being financed by the same man it's as good as a ring." He paused only for a moment before changing the subject briskly: "Have a word with Brixton, will you, and talk to NE. There's just a chance that pals of the Carters are going to stage a rescue attempt—it's the kind of thing Red would probably revel in, being the flamboyant type. Friday morning's the most likely time, when they're being brought up for the second hearing. Tell you what," Gideon added, "we'll warn the court to expect them late, twelve o'clock, say, and then get them out early. That way we should fool anyone who's got a rescue in mind."

"They wouldn't have the nerve," Bell said.

"You might be right," Gideon conceded, and caught himself out in a yawn. "What's the matter with me?"

"You've been working like an express train ever since you left the court," Bell said.

Gideon looked surprised.

* * * * *

It was the middle of the afternoon when a police launch of the Thames Division, dawdling along near the Pool of London, pulled near a little backwater, and the man on look-out called: "Easy now, there's something over there. Looks like an old coat, but it might have something in it." The launch swung slowly towards the backwater, little more than a big pool, the surface covered with green scum, orange peel, pieces of wood and old cartons floating near it, and the look-out man picked up his boat hook, leaned forward and prodded. "There's something in it all right," he said, and another man joined him and together they hooked the 'thing' and drew it towards the side of the launch.

Expertly, they hoisted the body aboard, and turned it over.

"That's Limpy Dale," said the look-out man. "Flash the Yard, Bill."

* * * * *

"So they killed him," Bell said heavily. "And I think I'm with you now, George. They wouldn't have killed him because he was going to turn Queen's Evidence; they know we've got enough to put them down for ten years at least. There's something in the wind, and an escape from Brixton is more likely than anything."

"Briefed everyone?"

"Yes. You laid it on with the court?"

"Yes," Gideon answered. "But I think we ought to send someone over to Brixton to have a look round. If Brixton thinks we're really serious, they'll be careful. Jim got much on?"

"No."

"Send him, then."

Just before Gideon left the office, at half past six that evening, Appleby rang up to say that if any attempt were made to release the Carter brothers next morning, there wasn't a ghost of a chance of its succeeding.

"Better not be," said Gideon dryly. He left the office, walked down to his car, sat in it for a moment or two reviewing the day again, and felt more satisfied than he had been for some time. The fact that Borgman was in Brixton and they were getting nearer to the nurse was easing his fears that the case would go sour.

Gideon had three late evening newspapers under his arm, and each front page screamed news of the arrest; there were photographs of Borgman's wife, his £40,000 home with its swimming pool and its private cinema, his yacht, even a picture of him getting out of his Rolls Bentley Continental. So far, no one had made any comment, but two newspapers put a lot of emphasis on the good works which Borgman did; his gifts to charity, his generosity to employees. These were the first whispers in a campaign to whitewash him, and no matter what any psychologist said, it was the kind of thing which could seep into the mind of a jury.

"But we're all right even if we don't find the nurse," Gideon told Kate, when they were in the back garden, trimming the privet hedge while she trimmed the lawn. "She's flashing her money about, and might have been blackmailing him, though. Or he might have bribed her to get out of England quick."

He went on clipping, and drawing at his empty pipe, until it was nearly dark, and was actually putting on his coat when he heard the telephone bell inside the house. Kate was already indoors. He went slowly and deliberately, as always, with the scent of new-mown grass pleasant on the air, and the perfume of night-scented stock wafted to him.

"It's O'Leary," Kate said.

"Thanks, dear . . . Hallo, Mike, can't you sleep?"

"George, a cable's just come in from Perth."

"Well?"

"The *Colombo*'s due in tomorrow, at Fremantle," O'Leary said, "and a woman named Jane Hoorn is on board. She joined the ship at Colombo just over a week ago."

"Well, well," said Gideon. "So we'll soon be able to talk to her." As if speaking to himself, he went on: "I'll telephone Delaney at Perth in the morning."

* * * * *

Twelve thousand miles from London, walking over the springy buffalo grass which was thicker than usual after the spring rains, Superintendent Delaney of the Perth Criminal Investigation Bureau approached his small yacht on the Swan River and was about to step into it when a car drew up and a tall man came hurrying.

"Tell them no, I'm out sailing," Delaney called.

"It's a call coming from Gideon of the Yard," the man called back. "It's due in half an hour's time; you're just in time to make it."

"Dunno that I want to," Delaney grumbled, but he turned away from the little boat with its furled white sail, looked wistfully at other small craft already moving swiftly before the wind, then went to the car. Five years ago, he had visited London and talked to Gideon, gone to his home, and been shown some of the sights by him. In half an hour exactly, he heard Gideon's voice.

"How are you, Eric?" Gideon sounded as clear as if he were only a few miles away. "Is the *Colombo* in yet?"

"Due this afternoon," Delaney answered.

"Will you go and see this Nurse Kennett—now Mrs Hoorn?" Gideon asked. "Ask her where she's got her money from, who—"

"Won't help you," Delaney interrupted promptly. "Her late husband struck it rich in gold, George; left her nearly a hundred thousand pounds."

Gideon said: "Oh," in a voice which sounded shocked.

"But I'll talk to her; I know what you're after," Delaney said. "Shall I ask her if she saw Borgman this trip?"

"Yes, do that," said Gideon.

* * * * *

At the time when the two policemen were talking over eleven thousand miles, Jane Hoorn—née Kennett—was standing near the stern of the great ship, watching the white wake, and the strange channel of smooth water in the middle of heavy seas. It never failed to fascinate her. She was alone, as she often was these days. Borgman was not even in her mind.

* * * * *

Gideon put down the receiver slowly, and sat back with his hands spread on the desk in front of him. Bell had been sitting with his ear fast to the extension, and knew everything that had been said. It was nearly nine o'clock, and Gideon had been in for half an hour. "Pity she's in the money legally," Gideon said. "It cuts out any likelihood that she's been getting money from Borgman." He was silent for a minute, then went on: "Did we get the official Fingerprints report on that stuff we found in Borgman's desk?"

"Absolutely clean of prints, Sammy said."

"Hmm. Oh, well. Let's look on the bright side," Gideon made himself say. "The Carters come up this morning. Nothing *could* go wrong there, could it?"

"Not a chance," said Bell heartily. "And there was a message from Hoppy just before you came in. They've found the swine who did in those girls. Uncle of one of them, who's been acting as sitter-in for a lot of children lately. No doubt about it this time—the night men at the lab checked everything. So that one's in the bag. Going over to the East End court yourself?"

"I'll leave it to Hugh," Gideon said.

* * * * *

The removal of the two Carters from Brixton Jail to the East End police court went off without any hint of trouble. The brothers looked depressed and miserable. There was no one outside to watch them. The police on duty at all approaches to the prison were tensed up for two minutes, but that was all. Two police cars followed the Black Maria, and the approach to the East End court was guarded just as well as the prison gates themselves.

The Division presented the evidence—that Red had been seen attacking Tiny Bray, that Syd had been stopped in the act of throwing Rachel Gully into Duck's Pool. Rachel gave her evidence in a subdued voice, and was obviously very nervous. Detective Officer Moss was in court, and took much more notice of Rachel than of the magistrate. The two men were committed for trial at the next sessions, after a dull hearing. Everyone had been keyed up until that moment; now there was a general air of relaxation, for the doors of the Black Maria opened, and the Carters, each handcuffed to a plainclothes man, stepped inside obediently. The doors were closed and locked behind them, and as the big black van started off, the two police cars which were on escort duty followed. The van turned a corner into the Whitechapel Road, and the first car followed. Until that moment, there was no hint of trouble, but suddenly there came a new, harsh note. A car started up, its engine roaring. As suddenly, two motor-cycles roared on the other side of the road, then swung across the stream of traffic.

The noisy car raced towards the first escort car, as if it were going to ram it. The police driver swung his wheel desperately, and mounted the pavement; and the second police car turned out to avoid it—and found the one with the roaring engine blocking the road. A dozen police were in sight, all behind the police cars; and they came running, two men blowing whistles furiously. Passers-by stopped to gape. The two motor-cyclists drew alongside the Black Maria, one on each side of the driving cabin, and clung on to the doors. One of them flung the contents of a bottle into the faces of the driver and his companion, and there was a stench of ammonia, while the two men snatched at their eyes. One of the motor-cyclists grabbed the wheel of the Black Maria and held it steady until his companion could climb in. The motor-cycles themselves had gone spinning and staggering on to the crowded pavement, where people were screaming with fear. Smoke bombs burst among the crowd, and in the road, and for a moment the Black Maria was cut off from view.

When it appeared again, a man was seen falling from it; and as he hit the ground another was pushed out of the driving cabin. The door slammed. Two men lay in crumpled heaps in the middle of the road, and the Black Maria screeched on.

* * * * *

Inside the van, the Carter brothers had slumped down on their seats, without dragging at their handcuffs and the men to whom they were secured, while the third guard sat at the back of the van, all thought of danger past. Then a shrill whistle sounded, giving a hint of alarm, and as it came, Syd smashed his clenched left fist into the face of the man to whom he was fastened, and Red butted his captor viciously in the nose. As the third man jumped up, Red kicked out and cracked him on the knee.

"Hold his neck," Syd said urgently, and Red thrust his free arm round the man handcuffed to his brother, forcing the bicep against the man's neck, and nearly choking him. Syd thrust his free hand into the detective's pocket and found the keys. Red let his victim go, and the man slumped down, half-conscious. There was a sharp click as the key turned, and Syd exclaimed triumphantly:

"Got it. Okay!" He pushed past his brother and went for the third guard.

* * * * *

"And it got clear away," Bell growled. He was much more affected by this news than he had been by the message from Australia. "It makes me sick."

"They can't take a Black Maria far," Rogerson reasoned, as if he found it hard to believe that a Black Maria had actually been stolen.

"How badly was the driver and his escort hurt?" asked Gideon. He had just come in from the Map Room, where he had been studying the car-theft figures, noting the places where the one-man one-boy garages were sited.

"Driver's got concussion and a broken arm, the other chap a fractured skull and bruises—both hurt as they hit the ground while the van was moving."

"What've you done?" Gideon demanded.

"The general call was out within minutes," Bell said, and Rogerson repeated: "They can't take it far."

"Got to admire their nerve," Gideon made himself say, but there was only bleakness in his expression and in his heart. "And we've got to face the fact that the Carters were much better organised than we realised. They must have had a dozen men involved in this, if not twice as many. Who's making a report?"

"Christy," Bell answered.

"Was that young chap Moss there?"

"Yes."

"He might have noticed something everyone else missed," Gideon said. "I'm going over there right away. Telephone Christy, ask him to have a sketch of the scene of the hold-up, and to try to get every point of distraction marked—where the smoke bombs fell, where they were thrown from, where the motor-cycles came from, all the usual stuff. I'll be there within half an hour."

"Sorry, George," Rogerson said. "The Old Man wants you to go along and see him."

Gideon said: "All right. I'll be there within an hour, then." He nodded and went out, and the two men left in his office, who knew him well, had never seen Gideon looking so bleak and so nearly vicious.

Gideon went striding along the corridor towards the first flight of stairs, and strode up them to the Commissioner's room. Colonel Scott-Marle, the 'Old Man' at the Yard, seldom sent for him unless it was a matter of exceptional importance, and then usually liked to have the Assistant Commissioner for Crime with him. But Gideon hardly gave a thought to the reason for this summons.

If the Carters got free it would give not only their gang but every professional crook in London a tremendous lift.

Gideon reached the outer office, and went in. Scott-Marle's secretary, a prim middle fifties, greeted him politely:

"Good-morning, Mr Gideon. The Commissioner would like you to go straight in."

As he tapped on the plain oak door which led to the Commissioner's office, Gideon paused for the first time to wonder what lay behind this summons. He did not know Scott-Marle well, and only once had he really been in close contact with him over a Yard problem; then it had been an administrative one. He heard a quiet "Come in," and went through. Scott-Marle was tall, very lean, rather aloof-looking, but that no longer put Gideon off; he knew that this man genuinely had the interests of the Yard and the work of the C.I.D. at heart. Scott-Marle gave a rather thin-lipped smile and, unexpectedly, shook hands.

"Sit down, Gideon. Cigarette?"

"Still don't use them, sir."

"Of course not." Scott-Marle did not sit down, and so put Gideon at a slight disadvantage. His hair was grey, crinkly, and cut close to the side of his head, and he had a very clearly marked parting. "I wanted an informal word with you about the Borgman case," he went on, "although after the Carter incident you probably aren't giving Borgman much thought. Is there any news of those two escapees?"

"No, sir."

"It would help a lot if we could catch them quickly, but

that won't be easy." Scott-Marle's expression suggested that this was just the luck of the game. "How confident are you about Borgman now?"

Gideon said: "I think there would be greater risk if we withdrew the charge than if we go ahead with it."

"What really persuaded you to fight for it?" Scott-Marle demanded.

Gideon said very quietly:

"The deciding factor was Borgman's relationship with his second wife and his present mistress. I've studied the personality of this man for a long time, Commissioner. He is going to great lengths to avoid an open scandal, and I don't think he would do that to consider his wife's feelings. I believe that he got away with one wife-murder, and a second was on the cards. If it had been known that he was estranged or on bad terms with his wife, anything which happened to her would immediately arouse suspicion. As things were before the arrest, an accident to her or death cleverly camouflaged as natural causes would have aroused sympathy and not much else."

Scott-Marle nodded, and was silent for a long time. Was that order coming? It would be a bitter failure, but perhaps less harmful than if evidence was offered, and Percy Richmond tore it to pieces.

"George," said Scott-Marle, unexpectedly, "I can see the quandary and sympathise with it, but it's no use blinking at facts. You pushed this charge through, even at the length of ignoring a Home Office instruction. If it goes wrong, they'll be after your blood. A year ago you ran into trouble with the Home Office over the economy drive they wanted you to make. This is your second clash with officials who could influence your future. If you win, there'll be nothing to worry about, but if the Borgman case is dismissed, you'll be the scapegoat."

There was a long pause before Gideon said, quietly: "I feel just as I did last year, sir. I believe we ought to go ahead, and my personal position shouldn't interfere with that. If we don't get Borgman now, we never will."

CHAPTER 13

RISK

GIDEON put his hand to his pocket and took out the big pipe, and smoothed it in his hands. Scott-Marle was standing by the window, looking at him, putting him at a disadvantage in exactly the same way that Gideon had Borgman, only two days ago. Scott-Marle was giving him plenty of time to think. Scott-Marle, he reminded himself, was completely loyal to his staff, and reliable: this was no kind of ultimatum from him. He was simply assessing a situation as he saw it. And it was seeping very deeply into Gideon's mind. It was not good to be forced to realise that what he did over one case could affect his whole future. He had earned that future, and was almost sure of what it should be.

"You do see the full implications, don't you?"

"Yes," Gideon answered briskly. "If I ever go higher it would be to take over the Assistant Commissioner's job, when Mr Rogerson retires."

"In three or four years at most, remember."

"That would need the seal of the Minister's approval," said Gideon, "and whoever is minister isn't likely to sign and seal it unless the permanent officials make the recommendation."

"That's right," Scott-Marle agreed.

"Has anyone put this into so many words, sir?" Gideon was beginning to boil.

"No, but many hints have been dropped," answered Scott-Marle. "I put it bluntly to the Permanent Secretary that Borgman's position and influence might be a contributory cause of the reluctance to go ahead. The answer was as blunt: if a prosecution against a man in Borgman's position fails the repercussions will be far-reaching. They won't do the Yard any good at all. He's right, of course. And he's afraid—like Plumley—that there will be a very big effort to get the case dismissed at the second hearing. If it is, there will be a lot of ridicule, a lot of talk about wasting public money. In other words, the Home Office wanted a certainty before we acted against Borgman, and they know we haven't got it. Well! You once told me that you couldn't make up your mind whether you wanted to become an A.C.—when you were *locum* it tied you to the desk too much. How do you feel now?"

Unexpectedly, Gideon found that he could smile.

"In the last five minutes I've decided that I want to become the A.C. very badly indeed," he said, and went on, his smile broadening: "Had a talk with my wife about it only a few weeks ago—you remember Kate?"

Scott-Marle said: "Of course."

"We decided that we would like the job," went on Gideon, and added rather ruefully: "I suppose the truth is that I'd taken it for granted that it would be available for me once Rogerson retired, and—but that's by the way, sir. I'm sorry I can't tell the Home Office people what I think about the suggestion that we should back down on Borgman, but if it's all right with you, I would like to be the chief police witness at the second hearing. There's all the old stuff about the accident and the brakes which had been tampered with; we're not entirely dependent on the killing by poison."

Scott-Marle began to smile quite freely. He moved away from the window, went to a cupboard in a corner, opened it and took out whisky, a syphon and two glasses.

"Let's drink to his committal for trial," he said.

Gideon said: "I'd much rather shake hands on it, sir. I've got to go over and talk to some of the Divisional chaps at NE about the Carter escape, and it wouldn't be wise to have whisky on my breath at this hour of the morning. They might think I was drinking to try to keep my spirits up!"

"What an awkward man you are for being right," said Scott-Marle. "Tell you what," he went on as he shook hands, "the first free Sunday, you and your wife must come and have lunch with us again."

"We'd like to very much," Gideon said, and was greatly cheered.

* * * * *

In the East End, there was a crowd of at least five hundred near the spot where the Black Maria had been held up. Traffic had been diverted to another main road, and only a thin trickle went through here, serving the local streets. The two motor-cycles were still on the ground, marked out with chalk; so were the spots where the driver and escort had fallen, and there were a few dark brown marks there; the blood of the man who had been worst injured. Uniformed police by the dozen stood at different points, and Gideon saw that three of them were standing by upturned boxes. Tall, military-looking Hugh Christy came hurrying towards him, and a battery of photographers followed.

"Glad you made it, George." Christy had the air and bearing of a Guards officer, and the voice of one, too; it was always a little surprising to discover that he was mellow and human. In fact he had never been in the Army, and his voice was acquired, but it had often been said that, because of it, he was the wrong man for this rough East End Division. Yet he thrived on it. "Can't wave a wand and catch the devils, can you?" he asked.

"Do my best," said Gideon. "What are the boxes for?"

"Covering places where we found smoke bomb fragments, fire crackers and broken bottles. We've got a few footprints, but I don't think they'll help. Both motor-cycles were stolen earlier this morning from outside a factory in Bethnal Green—they've been identified. The owners were at work all the morning, and had the keys in their pockets. They–you suddenly thought of something, George?"

"Just had a notion," Gideon explained. "How do these particular motor-cycles start? Key in the ignition, the same as a car, which is unusual." He was talking almost to himself. "The thieves must have had keys or they couldn't have risked taking the motor-cycles away—they might have been spotted if they'd fiddled with a piece of wire. There's a master key for most of these things."

"All pretty obvious, George," Christy said.

Gideon grinned. "Yes. Remember that memo asking for details of car thefts? The car thieves always have a master key so that they can start off without taking too many chances. We know the Carters have a lot of hangers-on, and we know the car thieves have a lot of men available, too. This was all laid on so slickly that—"

"You think they might be connected?"

"I just had a wonderful dream that they might be," said Gideon, almost wistfully. "Forget it."

"Not on your life!"

"All right," said Gideon. "Did you get that sketch plan made for me?"

"I put Moss on to it," answered Christy. "He's a useful man with a pencil, and deserves a chance. He's in an empty shop over there, doing it now."

"Let's go and see what he's done," Gideon said. He had to thrust his way through the crowd which was jostling for a closer sight of him, and Christy followed, looking rather like a sergeant-major. Gideon found himself wondering, as always when he was in the East End, how many of the people here were really well-disposed, and how many sympathised with the Carters. Ten per cent were against the police probably; certainly ten per cent would get a kick out of it if the police were discomfited. There was another fact that mustn't be lost sight of, either: by the daring of their escape the Carters would become heroes in the eyes of a great number of people whose attitude towards the police was no better than neutral. Many who read of the exploit in the evening newspapers would say off-handedly: "You have to admire their guts." Unless the Carters were found quickly, there was a good chance that they would win sufficient sympathy to be helped against the police long enough for them to get safely away.

Gideon stepped on to the pavement by the shop, and between a huge red FOR SALE sign and another which said

BARGAINS—MUST CLOSE, he saw Moss at a counter, another policeman with him; Moss was standing back and studying what he had drawn.

Then a stone smacked against the window, making it boom; and as Gideon and Christy swung round, another stone flew at head-height towards them. Gideon ducked. The stone smacked him on the forehead, just above the eye. He caught a glimpse of a man with his arm drawn back holding another stone ready to throw. Then a bigger stone came from one side and struck the top of Christy's hat and sent it flying. A man laughed; a girl giggled. Any moment the crowd would really start laughing, and the fact that blood was trickling down Gideon's forehead and into his eyes would make no difference. This had been laid on to make the police look silly, of course; and so to strengthen feeling for the Carters among the many people who seldom paused to think.

Gideon said: "Hold it, Hugh," and thrust himself into the crowd, carrying several people back by sheer weight, and making others sway out of the way. He could see the man who had been about to hurl the next stone, turning away from him now and trying to mix with the crowd. There was a hush, as everyone watched Gideon. He swung his left arm and brushed two youths out of his path, then reached a clear spot and ran ten yards, putting on a surprising burst of speed, rather like a charging rhino. The man he was after glanced over his shoulder, and missed a step. Before he could recover his balance Gideon had him by the shoulder. He spun the man round, saw a little, narrow, frightened face, then shifted his grip to the man's big ear.

"We'll go and have a little talk," Gideon said, and he held the man by his ear, thrusting him forwards towards the shop. The giggling started again, but it was no longer at him and Christy, and there was a different note about it. Gideon reached the pavement again as young Moss came out, pencil in hand.

"Here's the chap who threw the stones," Gideon said, and brushed blood off his forehead. "Know him?"

"I don't know him, but I recognise him," answered

Moss, with complete certainty. "He threw one of the smoke bombs at the Black Maria."

Gideon barked: "So he did." He let the man go, pushed him into the shop, spun him round, and said: "Where are the Carters? If you tell us now you might get away with it. If you don't, you'll get seven years for helping to hold up that van. Where are they?"

"I–I don't know," the little man muttered. "It's no use asking me; I don't know. I was given a fiver to throw that smoke bomb. I didn't know what it was all about." It would be difficult, if not impossible, to prove that he was lying, and Gideon sensed that he was up against a brick wall. "I was given an extra quid to throw stones at you coppers, too, but I never meant to hurt anyone. I was only trying to put the wind up you."

"Who paid you?" Gideon demanded.

"I dunno who it was," the man said mechanically, in his whining voice. "I'd never seen 'im before, I swear."

Gideon said: "We'll see about that." He turned to Christy, and said: "Will you fix him?"

"I'm longing for the chance," Christy said, and called a plainclothes man from the doorway. "Take this chap along and charge him with causing serious bodily harm to a police officer."

"I only just nicked him, look," the man protested, but there was little spirit in his voice, and he did not try to struggle when the police took him away.

Gideon was already studying the sketch plan which Moss had prepared of the district and, as he did so, he kept dabbing a handkerchief on the cut on his forehead. It was bleeding quite freely, but there was hardly any pain. Moss was certainly good: another Wills in the making. The diagram showed all the points of incident, and there were captions explaining exactly what had happened, routes to and from the spot, all details which would enable the police to cover the whole area thoroughly. But the best item of all was a note on a separate sheet of paper, naming all the known criminals who had been in the vicinity. Moss had seen some himself; and others had been named by different policemen. In that comparatively small area, eleven ex-convicts had been gathered; someone had made sure that feeling against the police would be worked up.

Christy came back.

"What do you think, George?" he asked. "Have all of these chaps pulled in for questioning?"

"Yes," Gideon said. "They'll probably all say they were paid to be there by someone they didn't know, but they knew all right, and one of them might crack. Who'll you put in charge?"

Moss stood quite straight-faced, but his eyes were pleading, and Christy said, with a plum in his cheek: "I'm a bit short of men, George—Moss might as well carry on with it. Eh?" That was a parade-ground bark.

"Should think so," said Gideon, and saw the glow of satisfaction in Moss's eyes. "The quicker each one of these chaps is questioned the better I'll like it." He turned to the door. "How's that Gully girl?"

"Much better, sir, thank you," Moss answered. "As a matter of fact she's staying at my place in Clapham. We've a big house with plenty of room, and my mother likes a paying guest or so. I'd like to prevent her from coming back to this part of London if I can."

"Good idea," Gideon said. "Get those jobs done quickly." He went out, with Christy on his heels, and as the door closed behind them Christy said: "He's your slave for life; I see how you do it now. Catch 'em young. Anything else on your mind, George?"

"I'm going to step up the pace on the inquiries about the car thefts," Gideon said. "You'd call it a hunch, but it's worth playing." He paused for a moment to look at the crowd. It was bigger than ever, and at the back men and women were jostling and pushing forward. What a sweaty, sticky, ill-dressed, ill-featured mob a crowd could look on a warm day. Most of the police work was finished and traffic would be able to start flowing soon, but the stone-throwing incident had brought more people here. Gideon recognised at least eight men who had been inside.

A lot had been going on under his nose, a lot more under Christy's nose, more still under the nose of Superintendent Hopkinson of the AB Division, which covered Fulham and neighbouring districts. Hopkinson, with his touchiness, might not be so good as he ought to be. Getting the right men in the Divisions was one of the Force's grave problems, and the time was probably coming when he should lay on a check of all Divisional C.I.D. branches. Slackness or inefficiency would do inestimable damage.

As he drove back to the Yard through the crowded narrow streets of the City, where Borgman had operated for so long, he wondered what agitation the Borgman arrest had caused. The City, so eminently respectable, so correct, so reliable, contained as many if not more criminals per head of population as the East End, but they were criminals in a different way. How many tax frauds were being planned at this moment? How many company directors were chiselling on accounts? How many little thefts were there, like that old man's, Borgman's cashier? Most of these were thefts which would be found out and dealt with without referring to the police; some might start another Samuel on the downward slide. Good out of evil? If it hadn't been for Samuel, the impetus to go ahead with the charge against Borgman might not have been so strong.

Gideon was held up in a traffic block opposite a narrow street where a sign reading: *Secure Safe Deposit* swung gently in the wind. A few years ago there had been a raid on that very place, a night watchman had been killed, Gideon himself had been injured. A few doors along was an office building with a dozen brass plates in the entrance; and in a second floor office one of the cleverest company frauds in his time had been carried out; he had actually made the arrest there, ten years ago. The trial had lasted for seven weeks. They were the days! He realised that he had enjoyed being out in Christy's manor —but when he became Assistant Commissioner, if ever he did, that kind of sortie would be denied him.

He was passing the Guildhall when he saw a Rolls-

Royce draw up, a man in livery open the door and, a moment later, the top-hatted figure of the Home Secretary get out and go towards the main doors; there was a Lord Mayor's Banquet for some special civic occasion today, and the Home Secretary was the chief speaker. He would not have the slightest idea of what was happening at the Yard, but he could make or mar Gideon's future.

Gideon drove on.

He got caught between two monster red buses, and the noisy engine of one of them was getting on his nerves; the fumes from the exhaust were worse than on most, too. But there was no way to edge himself out. He saw three people go up to cars parked in a side street and open the driving door without using a key; two go up and turn the key before the door opened. When were people going to realise the extent of their own culpability?

"Never, I suppose," Gideon said to himself, and then the traffic moved off. There was a gap on the other side of the road, giving him just room and time to nip past the bus that was nearly suffocating him with its fumes. He pulled out, and roared past; and two taxis, coming towards him, had to pull over sharply. As he passed one, the driver leaned out and bellowed: "*Ought to be in dock, that's where you ought to be!*" The second driver simply called: "*Bloody fool.*"

"Right, too," Gideon admitted aloud. Then he saw a City policeman watching him, saw the man's expression change on recognition, and knew that all thought of a charge of dangerous driving had flown from the policeman's mind. Then a man rather like Moss passed; with that prominent Adam's apple and looking a little simple. Moss would soon overcome that physiognomic disadvantage. It looked as if it were a case between him and the Gully girl. Good out of evil?

* * * * *

"I think I'll go out for a walk, Mrs Moss," said Rachel Gully, about the time that Gideon was turning into the Yard that day. "Is there anything I can get for you?"

"You could pop into the grocer's for a packet of custard

powder," said Mrs Moss. "Cyril does like a lot of thick custard, and I've run short. Don't be back later than four, will you?"

"Oh, I won't be as long as that," Rachel assured her.

She put on a green lightweight coat, tossed back her hair, and went into the street of terraced houses which was now becoming familiar; but it was like a new world for her. These houses were all three storeys high, and four times as large as the hovel where she lived with her mother. Every one was neat and tidy; each had a small front garden, most were freshly painted, all the windows shone, curtains were spotlessly clean, even the lamp-posts had been newly painted. The sun was shining almost directly above the rooftops, bringing out the colours in the late antirrhinums, the dahlias and the asters. The wind was gentle, and refreshing, and it gave her a strange feeling of contentment. She had never known such comfort or such kindliness as she had met with from Mrs Moss, and it was hard to believe that only a mile or so away her own mother was probably drinking gin, or leaning on a broom and talking to a neighbour, or waddling to the shops and trying to get groceries or meat on credit.

She would have to go and see her mother soon, of course; but she would never go back home to live.

She turned the corner. Just beyond was a short street of the same fine houses and, beyond, the High Street, with buses passing, traffic crowding, people thronging. Even the shops seemed bigger and brighter and crammed with more stock.

She saw a small car parked near the High Street, facing her; saw a man leaning against the wall of a house and reading a newspaper, as a great number of men did in her own neighbourhood. She had seen this man before, although she could not place him; and he did not appear to be taking any notice of her.

But he was.

He looked at her over the top of the newspaper, until she had turned the corner, and then he put the paper down and stepped into the kiosk. He dropped in his pennies, dialled, and waited, the cigarette drooping from his mouth like a little brown parasite. He listened for the dialling sound until, eventually, a man answered.

"That you, Alfy?" he asked, and the browned cigarette bobbed up and down. "It's Jake here . . . Yes, she's out . . . All okay for me to do the job?"

The man Alfy hesitated for what seemed a long time, then said: "Hold on, and I'll tell you," and put the receiver down in the little niche provided for it on the wall of the garage office. It was a small one, neatly kept, and although many of the papers on the little desk were marked with oily fingers, there was no dust or dirt anywhere. Most of the papers were held down by sparking plugs, spanners, piston rings and washers. On another, even smaller, table, stood a typewriter with a chair pushed back from it, and a girl's hand-knitted red cardigan draped over the back.

Alfy stepped into the repair shop behind the office.

There were a dozen cars in various stages of overhaul and, in the next archway marked *Paint Shop*, were five more, two of them being completely resprayed, one being touched up after an accident. Working with spray guns and wearing masks to keep their lungs clear of the sickly cellulose were three men—two of them a little taller than average. One of these wore a skull cap pulled right down over his head, so that not a vestige of hair showed; but he had a freckly skin of the kind that often went with red-haired men.

Alfy went to him. The other, taller man stopped using his gun, and the only hissing now was in the far corner, where a younger man was working.

"Red," Alfy said, "it's Jake."

"So what?" Red Carter asked.

"He wants to know if it's okay to do the job on Rachel Gully?"

"Boy," Red said, in a very soft voice, "you can tell him he can make any kind of mess of her he likes. Sure, it's okay. If it wasn't for little Raichy we wouldn't be out on a limb like this, if it wasn't for—" He stopped speaking, as if the words were choking him, and there was a glint of rage in his pale, greeny-grey eyes. His right eye was swollen, where he had banged it while fighting the detectives in the Black Maria. He had been here for two and a half hours, and still felt edgy, still hated the slightest movement at the doors. His brother seemed to be taking things more calmly: he always had.

"Okay, if that's the way you want it," Alfy said.

"Hold it," interrupted Syd. "I don't know that—"

"Stow it," Red said viciously. "That girl's a witness against me, the only witness. Get that? If she takes the stand she can put me away for a long time, but if she's in her box they won't have a real witness, and I can get away with mistaken identity on the murder rap. So don't try to hold anything up. The quicker it's done the better I'll like it. Go tell Jake, Alfy."

Alfy looked at Syd, as if for confirmation. Syd shrugged, and turned away. He wore a cloth cap and overalls which looked as if he had been getting more paint on them than on the car. As Alfy disappeared into the repair shop, he said:

"Why don't you stop worrying? They aren't going to catch up with us. We've a dozen places to go to, and there isn't anything to stop us now."

"That so?" asked Red, and put back his mask and picked up the spray gun again.

Alfy said into the telephone: "Okay, Jake, go ahead."

* * * * *

'Yes,' thought Rachel Gully, 'it's a different world.' She actually used the words to herself as she came out of a small grocer's shop, where an elderly man with a grey beard had treated her with old-world courtesy. The shop was old-fashioned, newly painted, and rich with fresh-ground coffee. Next to it was a dress shop, rather like the one where she worked, and she found herself comparing prices; they were ten per cent or so more here, so it might be a good idea to shop nearer her own home. She passed a policeman, who glanced at her but appeared to take no special notice, and her heart missed a beat. As she went by, she smiled to herself, not knowing how her face lit up, for she had no need to be nervous of policemen, although all her life she had been taught to be.

She went to a zebra crossing, and remembered the man leaning against the wall near the telephone kiosk. He wasn't there. She had never been so near real happiness. A motorist stopped to wave her over the crossing, and she reached the other side. As she passed one of several parked cars, she heard an engine start up, but she did not give the driver a thought. It was nearly four o'clock, and Cyril's mother liked her cup of tea at four. So she hurried.

As she neared the corner, she heard a car coming behind her, but there was nothing alarming in that. She reached the corner and hesitated, looking round before she crossed this road. The car was on the other side and looked as if it were going straight on. Out of the corner of her eye she saw another man walking after her, and with a flare of alarm she recognised him as one of the Carters' men.

She stepped into the road hurriedly—and heard the engine roar.

She looked round, to see the car swinging towards her, and she felt sure what was going to happen. She sprang forward in a desperate, despairing effort to save herself. The roar of the engine seemed deafening, she could almost feel the thud of the car against her body. She heard different sounds, as of a man shouting, a thudding, a shrill, high-pitched noise, a police whistle. Then she kicked against the kerb, tripped up, and sprawled headlong in the road, with the car almost on her.

She saw the face of the driver, his lips parted, his eyes staring, as if his fear was as great as hers. The whistle kept shrilling. The shouting grew louder. The car swung past her, and something seemed to snatch at her ankle, causing a sharp pain.

CHAPTER 14

MISSING MEN

GIDEON PUSHED an empty cup away from him as the telephone bell rang, picked it up and announced himself, and went on reading the top report of several that had come in during the afternoon. It was half past four. He sat with his coat off, perspiring a little, but not consciously hot.

"Mr Hooper of ST Division would like a word with you, sir."

"Put him through."

"Yes, sir." Gideon finished reading the report, scribbled: '*Check with Northern Ireland*,' and then heard the broad Dorset burr of Hooper of ST. He tried to think of anything on in that Division, south of the river, which would warrant the call, could think of nothing, and thought gloomily that it must be a new job: Hooper wouldn't call him about a trifle. "Hallo, Sam," he said. "Don't you think I've got enough on my plate?"

"Never known anyone up there overwork yet," retorted Hooper. "Thought you'd want this at once, George. There was an attempt to run down Rachel Gully. You know, the—"

"She hurt?" Gideon asked sharply.

"Sprained ankle. A wheel took off the heel of her shoe."

"Get the driver?"

"No. It was a newly painted Hillman Minx; they're two a penny. Our chap watching the girl managed to distract the swine; if it hadn't been for that she'd be a goner. She says she's seen him before with the Carters, but doesn't know his name. I've got a call out for the car, and a description of the driver—he'd been seen lounging by a telephone kiosk earlier."

"Did your chap get a good look?" asked Gideon.

"Yes."

"Can you spare him for an hour or so?"

"I know, I know," said Hooper. "Will he come up and look through the Rogues' Gallery? Yes—want him right away?"

"Please."

"You'll have to pay him overtime, he's done his stint today."

"You can afford that," Gideon said. "What's his name?"

"Watson—George Watson."

"Have him go straight to the Gallery. I'll lay it on," said Gideon. "Any tyre marks, or anything?"

"It's all being taken care of, and as soon as I've some photographs or anything else worth seeing, I'll call you."

"Thanks," said Gideon, and rang off; and heard Bell saying into another telephone:

". . . yes, in about half an hour, a man named Watson, from ST. Give him all the help you can." He rang off in turn, and said: "See, I'm learning to do what you tell me before it occurs to you. Well, you're right."

"That's a change. What about?"

"The tie-ups between the snatch of the Black Maria and the car thefts," Bell said quietly. "It was all so slick. Only expert drivers could get away with it, and after this job we know that Red can lay on cars and drivers. A newly-painted Hillman Minx fits, too—pity we couldn't get it and check the engine number to see if it was stolen." Bell was talking more freely than usual. "George, Red Carter's a bigger shot than I ever thought. How far do you think he really goes?"

"It's just beginning to worry me, too," Gideon admitted. "Anything in about the men in the Black Maria?"

"Bruises and shock, that's all." Bell found himself grinning. "You've got to hand it to them, George—they'd looked out the exact spot for the van; if it hadn't been for the tyre marks it would have stayed in that warehouse for days."

"I don't feel like handing anything to the Carters," Gideon said. He turned over a report, and found the next one was attached to a letter from the Surrey C.I.D. and headed: '*Suspected Horse Doping*.' He skimmed the letter and the general details. "See this about the Epsom job?"

"Yes. I could tell you the names of a dozen chaps who went down on the favourite on Saturday, George."

"Daresay," said Gideon, and read aloud: 'Running of Disc in the September Stakes exceptional and believed to be due to some kind of stimulant. . . . No indications of the usual drugs in blood or saliva except a faint trace of cortisone.' That's the latest pep dope for horses. How many outsiders have come up lately, Joe?"

"There are always some," Bell said, "but I'm not a horsey man."

"No." Gideon lifted a telephone. "Give me Mr Hamm." He had not long to wait. "Hallo, Hamm, got anything for me at a nice long price?" Gideon asked, grinning. He paused. "You're right, the Derby and the Grand National are my limit. Have you noticed any exceptional number of outsiders coming in first lately, though? . . . Yes, I had a feeling I'd seen them in the headlines more than usual. Will you check through and let me know? The morning will do. . . . Tomorrow morning, not next week! Thanks." He rang off. "He says he thinks that there have been an abnormal number of outsiders at the courses near London. Chase him tomorrow, Joe—we'll be lucky if we get a report from him this week, but it's worth trying. Heard anything from Brixton?"

"Nothing new," Bell answered, while making notes. "They're still sending food into Borgman from the Gourmet; he's getting VIP treatment all right. Wonder what his wife is really thinking?"

"I'm more interested in what Borgman's really planning," Gideon said, "and what Delaney's got out of that nurse. Nothing in?"

"No. Tell you what did come in," Bell went on. "This

blonde of Borgman's spent a lot of yesterday with Mrs B. and Cuthbertson, at Mrs B.'s flat. So they're not scratching each other's eyes out."

Gideon said, heavily: "Pity."

* * * * *

Charlotte Borgman hardly knew what to think, and hardly knew how she felt. From the time she had heard of her husband's arrest, she had felt numbed; and when she had seen him in the dock, and heard him remanded in custody, she had felt as if her world were coming to an end. A simple, honest woman, she had never been inside a police court before, and that had helped to unnerve her; but there was also the awfulness of the charge: that John had poisoned his first wife.

If he could kill one wife, what was there to prevent him from killing another?

Emotionally, she rejected the very possibility that he was guilty, but every now and then a sliver of doubt crept into her mind, cold and frightening: would the police have made such a charge if they were not sure of themselves? The newspapers carried the hideous story all the time: she had read about the exhumation, and the fact that the arrest had followed soon afterwards seemed to prove that the police had found what they had been looking for. Now that she was forced to make herself think, she realised how often John had been away from her in the past year or two. It was partly her fault; she was a poor traveller, always air and sea-sick, even short car rides could be unpleasant; and she had her world of the fashion *salons*, her hairdresser, her beauty specialists, her bridge and tea parties, her gooey cakes and cream. She knew that she was putting on weight, but it was very gradual, and it did not occur to her that she had lost much of her attractiveness.

Now, she began to wonder, and to study her face in the mirror of her luxury bedroom; study her figure especially, and the rolls of fat at the waist, the extra heaviness at the breast and the hips when she stepped out of her sunken bath in a bathroom. She had always admired the smoothness of her flesh, and liked the satiny feel of it beneath her hands, but in the few days since John had been arrested, she had begun almost to hate herself.

And she had begun to hate Cuthbertson.

At first she had turned to him as the only man who could really help her in this time of awful need, but there was a quality about him which she did not understand; he seemed to be trying to do something without telling her what it was, and he made it obvious that he had little regard for her intelligence.

He had much more for John's secretary.

Charlotte Borgman had met the girl several times, once in this Mayfair flat, with its main rooms overlooking Hyde Park, and all the beauty of the countryside in the heart of London. Clare Selby had come with an urgent message one afternoon when John had been off colour and had not gone to the office. A thin, cold type, Charlotte had concluded, the antithesis of what she was herself, absolutely different from any woman who would appeal to John.

This evening, she was expecting Cuthbertson and the girl to dinner. She could almost hear the solicitor's voice as he had said:

"One of the essential things, Mrs Borgman, is to establish the loyalty, the love and the honour of your husband and his absolute devotion to you. We have to show that it is utterly unthinkable that a man of his character could consider committing such a crime. That is *very* important indeed. We do not yet know whether this case will in fact be brought to trial, and I have hope—very sound hope—that we may be able to establish that there is no case to answer. One of the things to be established is your own personal friendship with Clare Selby."

"Why?" Charlotte had asked flatly.

"My dear Mrs Borgman, you know how damaging scurrilous gossip can be, especially in a large organisation where there is a great deal of jealousy. We must make sure that there is no possible risk that your husband might be considered—what shall I say?—unfaithful even in thought. Miss Selby—Clare—is a very attractive young woman; she is his personal secretary; it has been necessary for her to make certain journeys with him."

"And I didn't know," Charlotte had almost cried aloud.

"That is not uncommon, but since she is a very able young woman, and was promoted quickly, there is jealousy at the office, and there might be imputations of an *affaire*. Nothing could be further from the truth—you know that as well as I do—but in a case of this kind it is not always possible to rely on the truth being established. The police are extremely vindictive. That is already obvious, since they have taken five years to bring this charge—if they had had good reason to believe John guilty, they would have brought the charge before. I am convinced that someone with deep malice has laid false information before the police, and that is the kind of factor we have to combat. So, we must establish that you were fully aware of all the journeys that your husband made with his secretary, and it would be a very fine thing if it were made clear that you and Clare are great personal friends."

But she had only met the girl casually.

"The best way to establish that, I think, will be for us to have our discussions here, and for Clare to come and see you occasionally when you are on your own. After all, she is almost young enough to be your daughter!"

Oh, dear God: so she was: and she was slim and she had that beautiful complexion and the clear, calm eyes . . .

Clare Selby arrived that evening a little after half past six, ahead of Cuthbertson. It was a warm evening, and yet the girl looked immaculate and cool, without a hair out of place. She was wearing a model cocktail dress, too, and Charlotte had no doubt that it had cost nearer sixty than twenty guineas. Had she money of her own that she could afford such luxuries?

The maid announced her.

"Hallo, Charlotte," Clare greeted smoothly. She smiled charmingly, and came forward, and they touched cheeks. "How lovely you look tonight." *Does she think I'm an utter fool?* "It's unbearable to think that John is in that cell—utterly unbearable, isn't it?"

John.

"Yes," Charlotte said tensely. "I still can't believe it's really happened. There can't–there can't be any danger for him, can there?"

"Oh, not when the truth is known," Clare said. "Darling, could I have a drink? I'm absolutely parched tonight, and it's so harassing at the office—everyone seems to think they can do what they like now that John's away." *John.* She watched as the older woman poured out a sherry for herself, whisky and soda for the guest. "Thank you, that looks lovely." She drank, and then sat on the arm of a chair and crossed her slim, lovely legs. "Charlotte, I've had Mr Cuthbertson with me most of the afternoon, and obviously he's really worried about one thing."

"What–what thing?" Charlotte made herself ask.

"That secret compartment in his desk," Clare told her, and sipped her drink. "John had no idea that it was there. The desk wasn't new when he bought it, of course—it came from Lord Alston's study. Lord Alston is dead, and there's no way of proving that he must have put those things in the secret compartment."

"But John knew about them," Charlotte said miserably. "Just after he bought it he told me about the compartments. Why he actually showed me one of them!"

Clare was looking at her very levelly.

"Darling," she said with great deliberation, "you're dreaming. You must be. You see, if we can prove that John didn't know about the secret compartments in the desk, then it will go a long way to establishing his innocence. If it should be proved that he knew—"

"But he did know!"

"Did he?" asked Clare very softly. "Did he really, Charlotte? Do you want him to be sent for trial at the Old Bailey? Isn't it bad enough as things are? After all, you are his wife, and he is desperately in love with you. If he did want his first wife dead, it was only because he was so passionately in love with you. And you can help him more than you've ever been able to before. Mr Cuthbertson has been with him a lot, and John is positive that he told no one else about those secret compartments; you're the only one who could say that he knew about them. So—" The beautifully curved lips parted a little, as Clare paused before she went on softly: "You couldn't have known, could you?"

Charlotte could not answer.

"And there is another thing," Clare went on, swinging one beautiful leg. "There was, in fact, that family of John's wife. They all had a share in the inheritance, and several of them needed money pretty badly, didn't they?"

Charlotte's eyes lit up.

"I didn't know that, Clare. I hardly knew the family and John didn't talk much about them. Is that true? Were they in need of money?"

"Of course it's true," Clare assured her. "And that's one of the facts that Mr Cuthbertson is going to bring out. When it's known that there were other people who had the opportunity to commit the murder, and when it's known that anyone could have put that poison and the syringes in John's desk—well, Mr Cuthbertson says that the police case is bound to collapse. He says that the weight of public opinion in the City and in the Government is in John's favour. I mean, he's done so much good, and he's so well liked and respected. It would be a dreadful thing if anything were to happen to him; and you can make sure that it doesn't."

"If only I could," Charlotte cried.

"Charlotte," Clare said, and slid off the arm of the couch and came towards her, "there isn't any doubt about it at all. You and I can save him. Mr Cuthbertson is going to ask you certain questions tonight, and rehearse everything that will happen in the police court next week. It is absolutely essential that you should know exactly what to say. He's told me the kind of questions that the police will ask you, too, and I am going to practise them with you. You have to be absolutely word perfect, and I'm sure you will be."

After a long pause, Charlotte said huskily:

"I will be."

"That's wonderful," Clare said, and she slid an arm round the older woman. "John has always told me how lucky he was when he married you, and I can understand it now."

* * * * *

It was an awful situation, and in spite of what she had said to Clare, Borgman's wife did not know what to do. Cuthbertson wanted her to tell a barefaced lie, of course, but was that really surprising? If she could save John, if she could even help him, wasn't such a lie forgivable? It would only be a white lie.

Her duty was to her husband, remember: 'till death us do part'. But his first wife had said the same thing, and John had to her. Death *had* parted them.

Could there be any truth in the accusation? If she told those lies, would they be helping John and putting others, even herself, in danger?

* * * * *

It was about that time that a cable came into the Yard from Perth. It was decoded urgently and telephoned to Gideon.

It read, bleakly:

'WITNESS DENIES SEEING B. THIS TRIP STOP VERY TOUGH CUSTOMER STOP REGARD IT IMPROBABLE SHE WILL MAKE ANY STATEMENT STOP DELANEY.'

In the next three days, Clare and Cuthbertson visited Borgman's flat for hours on end. Gideon, who was told of this, and who was now quite sure that the police case would not be helped by Borgman's ex-mistress, had a shrewd idea that Borgman's wife was being drilled to give certain evidence. He was still not sure what line the defence would take, but was inclined to think that Cuthbertson would go all out to try to prove that there was no case to answer. The need for overcoming that plea preoccupied Gideon more than anything else, even more than the need for finding Red and Syd Carter.

He was looking through some newspapers in which

Borgman was being discreetly white-washed when his telephone bell rang.

"Gideon," he said gruffly.

"There's another cable from Adelaide, sir, being decoded now."

"Bring it in the moment you've done it," Gideon ordered, and was on edge for only five minutes. Then a messenger brought in the cable, typed with two carbon copies:

> 'STILL NO SUCCESS, WITNESS INTENDS FLYING TO SYDNEY TOMORROW STOP CAN ONLY HOLD IF NEW JUSTIFICATION AVAILABLE STOP PLEASE CABLE.'

Gideon picked up a pen, and wrote on a slip of paper: 'Cable to Delaney, C.I.B., Perth, W.A.: "NO ADDITIONAL JUSTIFICATION FOR HOLDING WITNESS." '

Then he looked sourly at the newspapers again. One had an article listing Borgman's many interests, his gifts to charities, and the general excellence of his character.

When Gideon got home, the same newspaper was folded at the same article.

"Did you read that, Kate?" he asked.

"Yes," Kate said.

"What do you make of it?"

"No one seems to want to believe he's guilty," Kate said quietly. "George, dear—" She broke off.

"Hm-hm?"

"What *is* there about Borgman? I even hear people in the shops and on buses saying that they don't believe he did it."

"I think it's the result of a clever whispering campaign," Gideon answered thoughtfully. "It started in the newspapers and it's being spread everywhere—on ships, trains, buses—the lot." He poked his fingers through his hair. "It's pretty rife at the Yard, too. If you ask me whether I think he did it, I'll walk out on you."

"What does Fred Lee think?"

Gideon said: "I'm not too happy about Fred. I fancy

he's afraid that he'll be on the losing side next week. I wish—hallo, wasn't that the front door?"

"I'll go," Kate said.

"You stay there." Kate was ironing, while sitting at a large ironing board, and Gideon heaved himself out of his chair and went to open the door. It might be someone for one of the children: the girls were in their room upstairs, reading a play for some local dramatic society; he could hear the murmur of their voices. He opened the door, and the light shone on Fred Lee's pale face.

"Talk of the devil," Gideon said, and stood aside. "Come in, Fred. Working overtime?"

"That's about it," said Lee, "and I'd like pounds for the hours I've put in on this job for the past week. Your youngsters home, George?"

"Come in the back, they won't hear us there." Gideon led the way, Lee came in and shook hands with Kate, who moved the ironing board so that she could push up a chair for the caller. Gideon went into the kitchen and came back with two bottles of beer and two glasses. He saw that Kate was assessing Fred Lee, and anyone could see the anxiety and the misgivings in the other's eyes. Gideon poured out, giving his own a bigger head than Lee's, and said:

"Here's health, Fred. What's worrying you?"

"The whole blasted case is worrying me," blurted out Lee, "and I can't get it out of my head that things run in threes, George. I've had two flops, and now I'm ready for the third. You seen tonight's *Globe*?"

"No."

"Take a look, then," Lee said, and took a folded newspaper out of his pocket and handed it to Gideon. There was a paragraph heavily marked in ball-point ink. Kate stood up, to read it over Gideon's shoulder, while Lee sipped his beer gloomily.

The Gideons read:

'*The late Lord Alston was known to have a passionate liking for secret drawers and hidden passages, and he took many of his secrets with him to the grave.*'

"Well, what does it mean?" asked Kate.

After a long pause, Gideon said softly: "It may mean that we can probably get him all right after all, Fred." He saw surprise spring into Lee's eyes, and puzzlement in his wife's. "It might not do what it's meant to do," he went on. "It's meant to imply that Borgman could have bought the desk without knowing about the secret compartment. If they could establish that, they'd have us on the wrong foot."

"I'm on the wrong foot already," Lee said.

"Shake out of it," Gideon said. "You got all the depositions in your case?"

"Yes—I've read 'em all until I'm sick."

"Get out those you got from Sammy after he'd had the desk gone over for prints," said Gideon.

"George, there were no fingerprints on the bottle, on the hypodermic syringes, or—" Lee stopped abruptly, and his eyes rounded comically. "*Gawd!*" he breathed. Kate looked sharply from him to Gideon, while Lee opened the middle section of his brief case, thumbed through some documents which were pinned together, and then pulled one out. "Here we are." He flipped over the pages. "Morphine bottle, two hypodermic syringes and the packets of morphia—negative. Compartment in which these items found—two sets of prints, neither identified. No way of saying how long they had been there; in a sealed compartment they could last for years. George," Lee said in a choky voice, "I must be going senile."

"You're worrying too much," Gideon said very tensely. "The desk still sealed up?"

"Yes, they're not going to take it to the court unless the magistrate asks for it."

"Nip over there, and get one of the *Fingerprint* chaps to go through all those compartments. Just one of Borgman's prints in one compartment will do. That'll be another hole sealed up." His eyes were bright and his voice as eager as a boy's, and Lee looked years younger. "Have another beer for luck."

"Haven't got time," said Lee.

When Gideon came back from seeing him off, he was humming; and Kate, looking towards the door and smiling, reminded herself that he hadn't hummed light-heartedly like that for a long time. She could still picture the delight with which he had spotted the flaw. She marvelled, as she always had and always would, at George's grasp of details and speed of thought, as well as his astonishing memory for trivial facts; or facts which did not seem to matter. He came in, said: "Why don't you put that ironing away and do it when I'm not home?" and immediately switched on the television. "All I want now is the news that Red Carter's been caught," he went on, as the set began to warm up. "Funny how often cases go in parallels. There's a kind of whispering campaign for Red and his brother, as well—started to do them a bit of good, too."

Kate said: "I'll just finish this shirt, and then I'll put it up. How do you mean?"

"The way they got away with the Black Maria caught the public fancy," Gideon said. The set began to whine, and he started to fiddle with it. " 'We hate their guts but you've got to admire their courage; hope they get a sporting chance'—that kind of attitude developed. And I was talking to Hugh Christy today. He's having a bad patch like Fred, although I don't think it will affect him so much. He says that there's a lot of talk in the Division—that Tiny Bray was a crook himself, and the worst kind, a traitor. So he deserved a beating up. And Syd Carter wasn't going to kill the Gully girl—they were going for a night out, and she changed her mind at the last moment. It won't do the Carters any good, but it shows the way the wind's blowing." He stood up, the volume right on the set now; and the picture began to form. "Oh, lor', it's that serial. Shall I switch off?"

"We might as well give it a trial," Kate said. "I rather like it, and—oh, *why* can't they let you alone for five minutes."

The telephone was ringing.

"Might be to say that Borgman's confessed or Red and

Syd Carter are back in the cell," remarked Gideon lightly. "I'll take it in the hall; you look at your young lovers." He closed the door and switched on the hall light, leaned against the wall and heard his two daughters upstairs, lifted the receiver, and announced himself:

"Gideon."

"Hallo, George," greeted O'Leary, and went on without preamble: "I've got a report here that I thought you'd like at once."

"Try me."

"The movements of Lucy Sansetti," O'Leary told him, "checked over four nights running. She's called for petrol and gone to the toilet while being served, at Mortimer's Garage, the Arches, Fulham, Bennett's Garage, New King's Road, Chelsea, and Butterby's Garage, Fulham Road. Tonight she's back at Mortimer's. Then there's the report you had in today from Wills. Three of these four garages are known to have been on the rocks last year, and now they're doing all right. It looks as if we've got something."

Gideon said: "Yes, Mike, it looks good. Have you put a ring round Mortimer's Garage?"

"Yes, it's in position now. All corners and approaches covered."

"That's the big place not far from the river near the football ground, isn't it?" Gideon said. "Right on my doorstep. Have some chaps up on the roof of the warehouse overlooking it. Have a couple of launches up to cover the river. Alert the Putney boys to make sure we can close the bridge and the towpath if we need to. Don't move in until I get there. If Lucy Sansetti comes out, let her get well away from the garage before picking her up. Right?"

"On the nose," O'Leary said.

CHAPTER 15

MORTIMER'S

Mortimer's Garage was a new one built on the site of an old, almost derelict place which had been there since the beginning of motor-cars. It had eight petrol pumps, each of them glowing with illumination at the top, each bright and shiny in red and yellow. Well-made drive-ins were on either side. There was a large showroom which stretched right across the pump line, with a drive-way to the repair shop and the paint shop behind. In a fenced-off area next to the garage there were forty or fifty new and second-hand cars, several of them marked: 'One Owner Only' or '3,000 Miles—a Snip.' These were exactly the kind of cars which might have been stolen and repainted and, if they were, then the owners of Mortimer's Garage were bloated with their own self-confidence.

Gideon pulled up at a pump marked 'Mixture' and a smart-looking girl in a white smock came from the showroom, where the cash desk was in a corner. A little Ford, Lucy Sansetti's car, was pulled up by the air installation, and a man was bending over the engine, as if looking for some trouble. Gideon knew that a dozen Yard and Divisional men were close by. Three of them were in a lorry which had parked outside a truck café a few yards along. One was parked opposite. The men on the nearby warehouse roof were out of sight, but ready to act at the first sign of action.

"Five, please," said Gideon, and opened his door and got out. "Check my oil and the battery, will you?" As the girl said, "yes," brightly, he strolled towards the doorway at one side of the saleroom, marked 'Toilet'. He saw Wills appear from the lines of cars for sale, with a sleek-looking motor salesman by his side, talking freely. Wills nodded. Gideon walked past the toilet door, towards the repair shop. He heard a man tapping, as if with a light hammer, and heard the hum of a battery charger and of a dynamo. A man appeared from the office just in front of Gideon, and asked pleasantly enough:

"You got a car in here, sir?"

"No, I—"

"The shop's reserved for customers with cars here only, sir."

"I daresay," said Gideon, and then Wills and another man jumped the fence which divided the drive-in from the parked cars. The little salesman gaped, and looked ready to shout. The man in front of Gideon was obviously scared. "What—" he began, and then Gideon shouldered him to one side, and another Yard man slipped into the office to make sure that no one could use the telephone.

In the repair shop there were half a dozen cars; a man was bending over an engine of one, like the mechanic outside. He gaped at Gideon and the other massive detective who strode in, and Gideon saw a youngster with a streak of oil across his forehead, wearing a pair of blue jeans.

"*Go and warn them!*" screamed the man whom Gideon had pushed aside.

A Yard man clapped his hand over this man's mouth. Gideon, Wills and two others rushed at the youngster, but suddenly he swung round, and dived towards the repair shop. As he reached it, Wills said reassuringly: "They'll walk right into our chaps at the back." The youth disappeared, shouting, and the door of the paint shop slammed as Wills reached it. He flung his weight against it, and forced it open a few inches. The others reached him in a stride, the weight of three big men was hurled against the door, and it began to sag open—until there was the sharp sound of a shot.

Wills drew in a hissing breath, and his body slumped. The other men, startled, took off their pressure, and the door was slammed. Gideon heard bolts being pushed home. And on the oily ground, eyes rounded and with a startled expression, Wills lay with blood oozing from a wound in his neck.

* * * * *

Reggie Cole had been enjoying himself that night, partly because of his love of engines and partly because Ethel would be here later. He now knew exactly what he was doing, and still had no compunction or regrets. He had stolen three cars, he had a hundred pounds tucked away, and he had been able to take Ethel to the places she deserved. She had a slap-up little flat, too, and her mother had gone away to the country. So far as Reggie Cole was concerned, everything was exactly right. The fact that there was some risk really gave an added zest to the situation, but he did not think seriously about risk. The day when he gave his mother a second thought was past, he told himself. He was on duty tonight, and had been told that at a sign from the man in the office he was to go quietly into the repair shop and raise the alarm.

Two men were busy in there, and he believed that they were simply doing overtime on cellulosing the stolen cars.

He had seen Lucy Sansetti go into the repair shop, and watched her for a moment. She was really something to look at, as dark as Ethel was fair, and with a heavier figure than Ethel's, but there was no doubt that she had the real statistics. She glanced round as she went inside, but he did not think she noticed him. When she had gone, he saw the paint shop door closed slowly on its hinges. It had not occurred to him to find out what was happening in the paint shop, or to wonder what the girl was doing there.

Then he had heard men approach, looked round, and seen the cashier in the arms of a big man while others hurried towards him: then the cashier had *screamed*: "Go and warn them!"

That was when Reggie realised that the big men were police.

He flung himself towards the paint shop, the door of which was ajar, and almost fell inside. One man was close to the door, without his mask. The other man, also without his mask, was standing with his arms round the girl, whose dress was off her shoulders and whose flesh looked startingly white. Outside, men came rushing, and the man nearer Reggie rasped:

"Close that door!" He sprang forward and pushed his weight against it, and Reggie did the same. There was heavy pressure, and the door seemed to give way; with a heave, he and his companion closed it again. The girl was backing away from the red-haired man, but Reggie hardly noticed that.

Then he heard the sound of the shot. He saw a man's hand appear near the ground, and disappear. The weight pressing against him eased. His companion said: "Now we've got it," and they banged the door home. The man dropped a bar into a slot, securing it, and then backed away.

Reggie had turned to look at the other. That was the first time he had seen the red-haired man without his mask, and he recognised him on the instant: this was Red Carter, who had stolen the Black Maria, and whose name had been all over the newspapers. Red had a pistol in his right hand, and there was a queer, twisted smile at his lips.

"So you had to shoot him," the other man said.

"That door was nearly open, we wouldn't have had a chance," Red Carter declared. "Okay, Lucy, over to the side door. Syd, you got the gun ready?"

"Yes," said Syd Carter. "How about our little pal here?" He was looking at Reggie, who still stood by the door staring at them. There was a thudding sound at the door, as if a battering ram were being used, but even that did not muffle the sound of his own pounding heart. He knew that death was waiting for him: that these men would kill him without compunction if they thought that it would help them. Red was already backing towards the door, and the girl had reached it. Were they crazy? Didn't they realise that the police would be outside that door, too? The garage was bound to be surrounded.

"You for or against us, kid?" asked Syd Carter.

Reggie fought for words.

"I–I warned you, didn't I?"

"That's right, you warned us," Syd said. "Okay, you're for us. You'd better be. Go and open that side door."

"B-b-but the cops—"

"Never mind the conversation, just go and open it," Syd said. He was picking up a curious-looking machine, rather like a very fat rifle which had been sawn off close to the stock; he held it like a gun, too, one end against his shoulder. "Open it, and tell them you'll give yourself up, see? Just let 'em in."

The thudding on the big door was heavier and louder, but there was no sound at the side; it was as if the police wanted them to go out that way. Reggie felt an awful constriction at his throat as he went towards the door. Red was standing with his arm round the girl, who was shivering as if it were bitterly cold. Syd was pointing the fat 'gun' towards the door. Reggie reached the door, his mind working fast despite his fears, and the sound of the shot echoing in his ears. Red still held the automatic; if he had shot one man, he would certainly be prepared to shoot others.

Red said softly: "Okay, kid. There are two cars outside, with one driver. You go for the black Austin, see, and Syd will come with you. I'll go for the Morris. You're a driver—all you've got to do is to drive Syd away and shake the cops off. We've plenty of places to hide."

Reggie gasped: "But they'll be outside!"

"And they'll come in. Like to know what will happen—"

"Shut up!" Syd ordered sharply.

Reggie saw the men exchange swift glances. He saw the gun in Red's hand rise. He saw it pointing towards him, and his breath was almost choking him when he gasped:

"All right, all right, I'll open it!" He threw himself at the door. It was bolted top and bottom, and there was a heavy iron bar dropped across it, to make it almost impossible to break it down. He pulled at one bolt; it slid easily. He glanced over his shoulder and saw the gun still pointing at him; and he saw Syd's, too; he had seen drawings of weapons like it, and suddenly he realised what it was: a flame gun.

Red mouthed the single word: "*Hurry*", and the gun was covering Reggie's chest, while the thudding at the main door was heavier, and soon it would crash in.

"*Hurry!*" Red mouthed again, and the third bolt came back; there was only the bar to lift. Reggie put his hands beneath it. It was very heavy, and not easy to shift. Reggie saw the two men standing on either side, and thought again of what would happen if the police streamed in. There were only a few minutes, perhaps only seconds, to spare.

He raised the bar.

He was sweating as if he were already roasting. He had seen what happened when flame guns were used, in pictures of army manoeuvres. He got the bar free from its slots, and held it higher, almost shoulder high.

Then the door was pushed against Reggie. There was a thud, as if the men outside had been waiting for this signal. He was pushed forward by the force of the movement, with the steel bar still in his hands. He saw each of the Carters ready to use their guns—and then something cracked inside him, and he knew that he could not allow this thing to happen. He hurled the bar towards Syd. Syd saw it coming and raised the flame gun towards him—and then the door crashed in.

As it swung back, the big door at the other side of the shop gave way.

* * * * *

Gideon saw everything that happened.

There was a gap between the double doors they had been trying to force. He saw the white-faced youth with the bar, Red and Syd with their guns, the girl by Red's side. One glimpse of the flame gun told him what they were planning, but the door behind the youth was already opening wider, and the police there would run right into that awful flame.

Then the youth flung the bar.

Syd Carter swung the gun towards him, there was a hiss of sound and a wicked tongue of flame, but the bar caught Syd across the shoulder, and he staggered and nearly lost control. Gideon, first to get into the shop, hurled himself across. Syd Carter still held the flame gun, and was trying to regain his balance. The flame had died down but was still hissing, and any man who got in the path of a single flare would have little chance of life.

Gideon saw Syd trying to swing it towards him; saw Red raising the automatic; saw Lucy suddenly strike at Red so that he lost his balance; and his own great hand struck Syd across the head, sending him flying and the gun clattering. Flame spat towards the floor, then snaked along the concrete a foot from Gideon, a yard from the boy.

* * * * *

Reggie Cole was sobbing. "I couldn't let them do it. I can't help it if I was ratting on them, I couldn't let them do it."

"You did yourself a lot of good, son," Gideon said soothingly. "Just take it easy." He watched as Syd and Red, handcuffed to a powerful man, were being led out. Lucy was not handcuffed, but there was a man on either side of her. In the street there was the bustle of excitement, the inevitable sensation as the police closed in. It had not taken long, but he did not want to live through a minute like that again.

"You'll have to come along with us," Gideon said to the youth, "but you can have someone to see you at the Yard, if you like."

There were tears in Reggie Cole's eyes as he said hoarsely:

"Could I–could I see my mother, please?"

* * * * *

"No, I won't be home until very late—you go to bed," Gideon said to Kate. There was excitement in his voice, and she knew that everything had gone well. "We got them cold; all right, but there are a lot of things that ought to be done right away. 'Night, dear."

He was in his own office. The door was propped open, and there was a continual parade of men in and out. Records found at Mortimer's Garage led straight to most people in the Carter mob; thirty in all in the East End, another fifteen at garages which were all controlled by Mortimer's, one of which was owned by the Carters.

Except for the anxiety about Wills, Gideon would have felt on top of the world. Wills was in the operating theatre at Fulham Hospital, and word might come through at any minute.

When Gideon left for home just after one o'clock, word about Wills had not come through.

When he woke at a quarter to seven next morning, there was still no news, and the fact hung over him like a pall, although he kept trying to convince himself that no news was good news. It was going to be a hell of a day. The second hearing of the charge against Borgman was enough in itself, and that could go on for anxious days, perhaps a week or more. Cuthbertson would leave nothing at all to chance, and Richmond would be ready to take advantage of the slightest weakness in the police case. Those prints might be the answer, but he didn't yet know.

Gideon left home at half past eight, waving to Kate who stood in the doorway, her smile hiding her anxiety. The real cause of anxiety was that he could not concentrate enough on the Borgman case; this day of all days he wanted his mind clear, but there was now this nagging anxiety for Wills, the disclosures about the car thefts and the Carter brothers buzzing in his mind. This was a day when he would leave the routine to Bell, although he would be at the office first, and he ought at least to look through the general reports. He saw the half dozen or so cars parked near the steps—there was always plenty of parking room at this hour of the morning—nodded to the men on duty in the main hall, and sensed that the news about Wills' injury had reached them: it was always possible to tell when there was anxiety at the Yard.

He pushed open his office door, and there was Joe Bell, sitting at his desk, coat off, collar and tie undone.

" 'Morning, George."

"Hallo, Joe. You're good and early."

"Knew you'd have enough on your plate," said Bell glumly. "Negative cable in from Sydney, Australia. Delaney asked them to try Mrs Hoorn, but she just says she hasn't seen Borgman for years and doesn't want to. We've had it with her."

Gideon grunted: "Anything else?"

"Our famous racing tipster is on top of his form," Bell went on. "Hamm's sent in his report on the dot for once."

"He would choose this morning. Let me see." Gideon slipped off his coat as he went to Bell's desk and read over his shoulder. " 'Seventeen outsiders have come up in the past three weeks, as compared with an average of three a week over the whole country'—not bad, Joe, he's done quite a job. 'Normal proportion outside the Home counties'—hallo, what's this? 'Over the past three years, there have been periodic periods,' "—he grinned—" 'when similar phenomena have appeared.' Hamm never could write a report. 'These occur at intervals of six to seven weeks and usually last for three to four weeks. There appears to be reason to believe that . . .' What he means is, it looks as if someone is pepping up outsiders, fixing a short period for it, and then dropping it so that it isn't too obvious. Okay, tell him to keep at it. They were too late with the last one, so the next outsider to win ought to have a blood and saliva test, and it had better be kept up until we have all the evidence we need. I'll talk to the Jockey Club." He hesitated. "No, we'd better have the Old Man do that; I'll ask him to fix it." He made a note to tell Rogerson that he would like to make this recommendation to Scott-Marle. "What else is there?" He hoped desperately to have news that Borgman's prints had been found inside a compartment in the late Lord Alston's desk.

"Hoppy's been on the buzzer," Bell answered. "He says he thinks that Mrs Robson knew all about Carslake killing and burying her husband, and he'd like to pull her in."

"He made a report?"

"No. He says he's afraid she might duck, and we don't want to give the Press another excuse for saying we're asleep."

"All right, if he's satisfied that we can make it stick, let him charge her." Gideon was studying the documents ready for the Borgman case, and then saw the report on the fingerprints inside the secret compartment.

'Still unidentified', it said; so they hadn't yet got the evidence they needed. Gloomily he read on. It was already nine o'clock, and the hearing would be on by ten thirty; he wanted to have a full hour briefing himself. "Anything else?"

"Got a nasty job out at Chiswick; looks as if a sixty-year old couple were killed by their only son; but it can keep," Bell answered. "Why don't you go into Rogerson's room? He won't be in this morning."

"Good idea." Gideon gathered up his papers, and asked almost casually: "Nothing in about Wills, I suppose."

Bell dropped his hands to his desk.

"Haven't you heard?"

"No," said Gideon, and felt his jaw going tense, fearing what Bell was going to say, and hating it.

"Thought Mike O'Leary called you," Bell said. "Wills died at half past five. That means the rope for the Carters."

Gideon gave one of his long pauses, and then said heavily: "Yes. Yes, it'll hang them all right." He knew that he had gone pale, and there was heaviness in his step as he went to the door. Wills had been really promising; one of the best of the younger men. In fifteen years' time he would have been a superintendent, or very near it. Last night he had been eager and on top of the world, aware that he had seized his main chance with both hands. One shot—and he was dead. He had a wife. He had two children, each under school age.

Gideon stood by the door, and asked: "Who's seen his wife?"

"Hoppy."

"Hmm. All right, Joe."

He went into the Assistant Commissioner's room, put a note on the secretary's desk in an ante-room, asking not to be disturbed, and spread out the document in the

Borgman case. It was at once simple and involved, and he examined every weakness he could see. At half past nine Fred Lee came in, and was obviously edgy, while both of them seemed to be brushed by the shadow of Wills' death.

There was young Moss, who had done much the same kind of job as Wills. Funny how it worked out. If the Carters had really wanted to kill for vengeance' sake, it would have been Moss. As it was, Moss and the Gully girl would probably make a match of it, and Moss would get to the top—or nearly to the top. He hadn't the weight needed for this job, but Wills had had plenty; Wills was going to be hard to replace.

At ten o'clock he said: "Okay, Fred, let's go."

* * * * *

As they drove along Regent Street towards Great Marlborough Street and the police court, they passed a tall, good-looking man wearing an overcheck jacket and grey flannels: the outdoor type to perfection. He was going into a jeweller's. In his pocket was a small capsule of cortisone solution, similar to that used at Haydock Park only yesterday. He bought a tie pin that had caught his fancy, and left when Gideon and Lee had parked round the corner and entered the court room. He went to his flat, and had been in for hardly five minutes before the telephone bell rang.

"Kingsley speaking," he answered.

"How did it go yesterday?" Soames asked, without mentioning his name.

"Easy as ever," Kingsley said confidently.

"Good. We're going to lay off for a few weeks, but it won't make any difference to your salary. . . . No, nothing's wrong, we're just being careful. Come to the club in the usual way, and make sure you show yourself in the stables; it will be a good thing if you're around when nothing unusual does happen. Understand?"

"Perfectly," Kingsley said. "Thanks, old chap."

When he rang off, he lit a cigarette, picked up a copy of the *Racing Calendar*, and sat in an easy chair with his feet up. He felt that he was made for life.

CHAPTER 16

SECOND HEARING

GIDEON'S PRESENCE in the court for a second time obviously caused a stir. The Fleet Street men present knew that it meant that he was committing himself, and although he might not give evidence, his name would be headlined more than Lee's, or any of the officers involved. Every seat was occupied, every square foot of space was used. Gideon looked round, sensing the excitement and noting that by far the coolest person here was Clare Selby. Borgman's mistress sat next to Borgman's wife, who looked a little thinner and rather pale—as if she had deliberately not put on rouge and used very little lipstick that morning.

The magistrate had dealt with two vagrancy cases, and conferred with the clerk in his usual rather ostentatious way. Gideon had an uneasy feeling that, without knowing it, Calahan might be biassed in Borgman's favour. There was the anticipated throng of solicitors and barristers, a sight seen only occasionally at a police court, all conferring, all giving the impression that they were absolutely sure of themselves. Plumley was there, looking rather anxious, with other solicitors from the Public Prosecutor's office; Gideon had advised playing the prosecution on a soft pedal, and trying to get the defence to put on the pressure.

Lee was staring at a short, stocky man with a ruddy face, a man who looked as if he spent half his time out of doors, and who had very clear, pale blue eyes. This man glanced up suddenly, and caught Lee's eyes. That was undoubtedly deliberate; and that was the kind of tactic that Percy Richmond would always employ. Richmond glanced next at Gideon, who stared at him blank-faced, and then turned for a word with Cuthbertson. Gideon looked at Lee.

"The devil's gunning for me all right," Lee said. "Know what I think?"

"Tell me."

"They're going all out for the kill today. They don't want this to drag on; the longer it drags on the more we can say and do. They'll try to get the case dismissed today, if they've a ghost of a chance."

"Have a job," Gideon said.

"Wouldn't like to say," said Lee. "I think they've got something up their sleeve, too. They wouldn't be so cocky if they hadn't. I'm as worried as hell, George, and yet—"

"Forget the worry," Gideon urged, but the words seemed empty, even to him. "And yet what?"

"There's still something about the morphine bottles," Lee said. "They're Zentens, I've checked that, and yet—it's like something on the tip of my tongue. I hope to God I can get it off when Richmond's tearing my guts out."

Gideon thought: 'I hope I did the right thing by giving him this job.' He made himself study the magistrate's sharp features, and then waited for the door from the cells to open; Borgman was a few minutes later than expected, and there was a hush of expectancy; this pause had probably been laid on for effect. Cuthbertson was regally confident, and Richmond looked as if he were in a mood to brush aside all opposition.

"All this nonsense," he seemed to be saying. "We'll soon settle it."

Then the door to the jailer's office and the cells opened, and a large, elderly police-sergeant came in, with Borgman; and two men followed.

"Number one remand, sir, John Borgman," the sergeant said.

"Very well," Calahan said, and nodded. "Is there any change of plea?"

Richmond stood up, smiling, robust, and put his hands to the lapels of his coat.

"I appear for Mr Borgman, Your Honour, and the plea of Not Guilty remains."

The rustle of interest could not be checked, and Gideon found himself watching Borgman's studied movements, almost admiring his immaculateness and his bearing. Borgman stood in the dock with all the confidence in the world. He glanced immediately at his wife, gave her a smile that was positively radiant, paused, glanced and nodded to his secretary, and then placed his hands on the rails of the dock.

The performance had begun.

When Lee was in the box giving formal evidence of the arrest, Richmond was fidgeting as if he could not wait to get at the witness. So this was to be a real offensive—the usual tactics for the defence and an indication of absolute confidence. No wonder Lee was already on edge. Lee looked more round-shouldered than usual, and unsure of himself, and Gideon felt his own doubts rising fast. He should have been in that box. He should have been ready to give Richmond just as good as he got. As commander, he couldn't be there, but it needed a man with more weight and confidence than Lee.

". . . may it please Your Honour, I would like to ask the witness some questions—vital questions to the accused, who is, of course, completely innocent of these—" Richmond paused, as if he were meaning to say 'ridiculous charges', but stopped in time and just said 'charges'.

"Proceed," Calahan said.

"Thank you, sir. Now—" Richmond glared at Lee, and waited until the slight buzz of excitement had died down, and then lowered his voice so that it had a growling note: histrionics usually reserved for the jury, Gideon knew, but effective here because in a way he had already managed to suggest that it was Lee, not Borgman, on trial; that was the secret of the man's mastery. "You are a chief superintendent of the Criminal Investigation Department of New Scotland Yard, and you have often made arrests of this nature before. Is that so?"

"I have often made arrests," Lee said, calmly enough.

"Please listen to my questions. I said: 'Of this nature'."

"I heard you."

"Have you ever made arrests of this nature before?"

Calahan said: "It would perhaps clarify the question if you were to elaborate what you mean by 'this nature', Mr Richmond."

"I think the witness is fully aware of my meaning, Your Honour, but I shall be happy to explain to the court," said Richmond. "This was a somewhat unusual arrest. It was an arrest which followed a remarkable and a grossly improper action by the police—by this witness. It was done in such a way that I imagine that it must have been *without* the approval or the knowledge of the Assistant Commissioner for Crime."

Calahan said: "Mr Richmond, you will please elicit your facts by questions."

"Fool," muttered Appleby, who was next to Gideon. "He shouldn't have given Richmond even half a chance."

Richmond said: "Certainly, your Honour." He stared at Lee again, and Gideon saw that Lee's hands were clenched tightly by his side. "Superintendent, did you visit the general offices of Borgman Enterprises Limited on the morning before you made this—ah—charge?"

"Yes."

"On what business?"

"I was investigating a complaint made by the accused about shortages in certain accounts."

"Did you find those shortages?"

"Yes."

"Did you report to Mr Borgman?"

"No."

"Why not?"

"He wasn't there," Lee said.

"You mean, he was not in the general office?"

"As far as I knew, he was not on the premises."

"Do you know where he was?"

"I understand that he was in Paris."

"Did you go into his private office?"

Lee hesitated, and before he could answer, Richmond thundered:

"*Did you?*"

"Yes."

"Knowing that he was not there?"

"Yes."

"Why did you go?"

Lee said: "I put my report on his desk."

"Is that all?"

Lee paused again, and Richmond thundered: "Is that all, Superintendent?"

Lee said thinly: "No."

"What else did you do?"

"I examined his desk."

"For what purpose?"

"To find out what was in it."

"I see," said Richmond, and his voice was pitched high with scorn. He turned to the magistrate as he might to a jury, and said: "We have come to a pretty pass when an officer of the law, a man whose duty and obligation it is to carry out the law in all its aspects, admits in open court that without a search warrant, without permission, without excuse, he entered the private office of a citizen who has his full legal rights, to pry—that is the only word—to *pry* into his personal belongings. *Did* you have a search warrant, Superintendent?"

Appleby whispered: "It's going to be a bloody massacre."

"No," answered Lee.

"Did your superiors know that—"

Gideon stood up, the floorboards creaking as he did so and making everyone look round at him.

"The search was made on my orders. Mr Lee had no choice but to obey," he rumbled.

Richmond snapped: "When you are called to the box it is time for you to admit your own improper instructions to a subordinate. Not until then."

Calahan said, rather stiffly: "I think I can keep order in my own court, Mr Richmond, thank you. Do I understand that you wish to be called to testify, Commander Gideon?"

"If you think it necessary, sir."

"I see. Very well. Please do not interrupt the proceedings again. Now—you may proceed, Mr Richmond."

Richmond said: "Thank you, Your Worship." He paused and raised a hand, pointing at Lee, and said in a voice pitched on a much lower key: "Is it true that you carried out this search, this so-called repugnant duty, at the behest of your superior officer?"

"The bloody fool won't deny it, will he?" Appleby whispered.

"Yes," Lee said.

"Very well. What did you find in this desk?"

Lee hesitated again, and rubbed his chin. Richmond did not hector him this time, just waited; but he struck a posture which created an air of ridicule that might be even more damaging than a swift repeat of the question. For the first time since the hearing had begun, there was a hush in the court, and even Calahan was staring expectantly at Lee, with what might have been a hint of sympathy in his expression.

"Could it be that you have *forgotten* what you found?" asked Richmond softly.

A woman tittered.

Lee said: "No."

"No what?"

"No, I haven't forgotten what I found," Lee said.

"*What's the matter with him?*" whispered Appleby, and the clerk to the court glanced up irritably, but it would take much more than that to intimidate Appleby, who went on: "He's looking a bit queer to me, George. Not going to collapse, is he?"

"Shut up."

"Then perhaps you will be good enough to inform the court what you found," Richmond jeered.

"Yes," answered Lee. His shoulders seemed less rounded and he was standing more upright. "I found four secret compartments."

"Indeed. Had you been forewarned that there were secret compartments?"

"No."

"Indeed? Yet you found them—just like that?"

"They were quite difficult to find."

"So you made a very thorough job of this illicit search," Richmond sneered. "No doubt you believe that the end justifies the means. What did you find in these compartments?"

"Three were empty."

"And what was in the fourth?" Richmond raised his voice and then, as Lee appeared to gather himself to answer, he said: "Were you alone during this search?"

"No. I had a detective sergeant with me."

"Was there a third party present?"

"No," Lee said, and smiled. "Two was plenty." His manner had changed so markedly that even Richmond looked nonplussed, and Appleby was rubbing his fingers together agitatedly, while there was tension among the Fleet Street men, and a tension in Cuthbertson as well as among Borgman's friends. Until that moment Borgman had been almost forgotten, but Lee glanced at him as he smiled, and suddenly Borgman was right in the middle of the picture. His wife looked as if she would faint; his mistress was biting her lips.

"Will you tell the court what you found, without further delay, please."

"Yes," said Lee. "I found two hypodermic needles, one phial of morphine preparation for injection, sufficient to kill—"

"Are you a qualified medical practitioner?"

"No."

"Your Worship, may I ask that the witness does not attempt to give evidence which would be more reliably given by a medical witness?"

"Superintendent, we would prefer not to have your opinion about how many persons might or might not be killed by this preparation which you found." Calahan glanced round at a court which seemed stunned by the announcement; the only sound came from two reporters who were squeezing their way out of the court, obviously to get to a telephone.

"Thank you," Richmond said. "Superintendent, have you completed the statement of your discovery?"

"There was a supply of a chemical I believed to be morphine in liquid and in powder form."

"Is that all?"

"Yes."

"Did you carefully examine all the articles?"

"Yes."

"Did you find any of Mr Borgman's fingerprints on any of them?"

Lee glanced at Borgman again, and Borgman was more tense than he had been, giving the impression that he was worried; and that Lee worried him. Richmond had lost the edge of his attack, too, and that could only be because of the change in Lee's manner.

"I'm not an expert witness," Lee said, and there was a guffaw of laughter from someone in the crowd, a giggle from another part of the court. Calahan did not even look up reprovingly.

"You are a police officer of long standing, a senior official of the Criminal Investigation Department. Presumably you know a *little* about your job?"

"Didn't think you wanted me to pose as an expert," Lee retorted.

Appleby's grin was taut, and his hands were clenched together on his knees.

"*What's happened to him, George?*"

Gideon said: "We'll see."

"As a police officer of some experience, did you examine the articles found, and did you find any of Mr Borgman's fingerprints on them?"

"No."

"Were there any prints?"

"One or two unidentifiable smudges, that's all."

"Does that not imply that the articles had not been wiped clean of prints, and, further, that they might have been in that compartment for a long time?"

"Didn't know you were an expert," Lee said perkily.

"Is it within your range of knowledge that fingerprints

last for an indefinite period when in an enclosed space?" Richmond demanded. "And"—he pointed a finger and and raised his voice—"are you aware that the previous owner of this desk suffered acutely from a most painful condition, and frequently injected morphine into himself so as to ease the pain?"

"God!" gasped Appleby.

"Oldest known one was found in the tomb of a Pharaoh," said Lee, "and, according to my colleagues at the Yard, in certain circumstances they might be preserved a lot longer than that." Lee was positively coasting along, and it seemed unbelievable, for Richmond would certainly produce a witness that the late Lord Alston had made a practice of injecting morphine into himself.

"So what you found in that secret compartment could have been there for many years during Lord Alston's ownership," Richmond said. "One can presume—"

"Can't presume anything in my job," interrupted Lee. "You have to deal in facts."

"Precisely. And I am going to demonstrate the fact that my client, the accused, could not have known of the existence of those objects, because they were there before he acquired the desk, and because—"

"Couldn't have been," Lee interrupted.

Appleby said: "*He's gone mad.*"

"*If he has, let's all go mad,*" Gideon whispered.

"*What* did you say?" demanded Richmond, almost shrill.

"The accused bought the desk seven years ago. I've seen the invoice and the ledger entry of the purchase," Lee declared. "The morphine solution was prepared and packed just under five years ago. It was prepared by Zentens. They use phials of a different shape and size every so often," Lee went on. "I know, because I was handling a morphine poisoning job about the time that the first Mrs Borgman died. In that case there were two phials, and I went to Zentens' and found out the difference between them. The kind found in that secret compartment was not manufactured until 1955. So this must have been put in after Mr Borgman bought the desk."

"*George*," breathed Appleby, "*we've got him.*"

* * * * *

"They'll fight for it," Gideon said, later that afternoon, after the hearing had been adjourned. "Might go on for a week now, but we'll get him. When we come out with the result of the exhumation—"

"It'll floor 'em," Appleby exulted.

"On top of this, yes," said Gideon. "Well, Fred, how does it feel to have turned the tables on Percy?"

"It was the great moment of my life," Lee said, "and I don't mind admitting I had a job to stop myself from grinning like a Cheshire cat. Funny thing, I puzzled about that bottle for days—felt sure there was something I knew about it. And it came to me when Percy was tearing me to strips. As a matter of fact I was thinking I would give my pension to be able to wipe the smirk off his face, and—well, no point in talking any more about it. George, if it hadn't been for you—"

"Forget it," Gideon said.

He was quite sure that Borgman would be committed for trial, as sure as he could be of the result of the trial itself. Plumley said as much after the adjournment. But he was puzzled. In the excitement, logic had been overlooked, but would a man of Borgman's intelligence leave incriminating evidence in his desk? It didn't make sense. He could have got rid of it any time—

"If he'd known it was there," Gideon said, and then his voice rose. "My God, *if* he knew. If he didn't, then who put it there?"

* * * * *

"The only person who could have put the morphine and the syringe in the desk was Nurse Kennett," Borgman said. "If you could find her . . ."

"Mr. Borgman," Cuthbertson interrupted, "I don't think we should try to bring her into the case as a witness. Remember, she would be closely cross-examined. To help you, it would have to be implied that she was a guilty party. Under such pressure, do you think her testimony would help you?"

After a long pause, Borgman muttered: "No."

"Didn't she once threaten blackmail?"

"Yes," Borgman admitted, "but soon afterwards she got married, and—" He broke off.

"She had left behind her the tools of blackmail—that much is evident," Cuthbertson said. "I will do everything, everything I can, and so will Mr Richmond. If we can only put reasonable doubt into the minds of the jury, we will win the case. Be sure of that."

* * * * *

Gideon felt quite sure that the Crown would win.

The Carter case was an even greater certainty.

The young van driver who had taken such risks with the Carters had made a statement, and would not be charged, but there were dozens of charges pending, and the finishing touches to be given to the whole case. There was the race doping to follow up. There was the matricide and patricide case—one of the ugliest there could be. There was the Robson case to see through: Hoppy wanted watching on that. There was Moss to talk to—and Christy, too. Christy ought to recommend promotion for Moss pretty soon. There was the whole of London's crime still on the doorstep; the hangover of the old and the appetisers for the new. But the risk had been taken and the future assured. Tonight he could go home early, to Kate.